Anastasia's
BOOK OF DAYS

CINDY MAYNARD

ISBN: 978-1-4834-7292-8 (sc)
ISBN: 978-1-4834-7291-1 (e)

Library of Congress Control Number: 2017910800

Front cover photo courtesy of: Rehs Galleries, Inc., New York City.
Artist: Jules Breton, 1858,
La petite charcouterière

Lulu Publishing Services rev. date: 7/17/2017

ACKNOWLEDGMENT

I would like to thank my long-suffering husband, Bob Maynard, for being a thoughtful reader, and for his unwavering support. Sincere thanks also go to Danielle Devereaux-Weber, my editor, whose eagle eye made this book immeasurably better. Her enthusiasm for this project made the effort so much more enjoyable. Finally, I must thank Christiane Hatz, my beloved "German sister," a family member who still lives in the town where Anastasia spent her life. She was invaluable in correcting the German words, names, and places. Thank you, Christiane, for showing me the beauty of the land during my visit and for your inspiring spirit.

PROLOGUE
1873

I know my days are few. When I sleep, all my loved ones come to me, whispering, beckoning me to join them. They promise they will help me cross over. The next life now seems more immediate to me than the present day. I am sitting at the second-story window of the house where I was born. The light filtering in is a faded, sallow yellow. I couldn't say if this color arises because the light passes through the wavy, dirty window glass or because it enters through my cloudy eyes. I absently finger the pages of my book of days. For over sixty years, the pages of my book have held the joys and secrets of a girl's heart. People now look at me as an aged crone, as if I have always been old and diminished. But I was not always as I am now. I have had a long life filled with long stories. I am not diminished. I am amplified, enlarged by the fullness of my time on this earth. I am a vessel filled to overflowing with all that has gone before and a beacon for all who will come after me. I thought I would burn the book that recorded my days or tuck it into a desk drawer, never to be seen again, or take it with me to my grave. But now, as I approach the end of my story, I see that I am a time-travel machine. Through me, the past, present, and future blend. I feel the presence of women not yet born, generations of women—women who also will feel the past, present, and future merging in their own lives. I am, as they are, a conduit through which the generations are born and reborn. These are my stories.

CHAPTER 1

MAMA'S GIFT

WINTER 1805

The snow lay deep and pure on the steep hills above our town. Yesterday's swirling wraiths of snow had calmed and settled into sweet, soft pillows sprinkled with glistening sparkles. The air stung my lungs, making me gasp with every inhalation and puff out little bursts of steam on every exhalation.

"Make yourselves useful, you two! Gilly, stay out from underfoot! These Belgians are good, calm horses, but if they don't see you, they'll step on you," Father warned. "You'll be sorry then!" He turned in my direction. "Anastasia, bring me the bag of oats. They'll have a treat after they've helped us find the perfect tree." Father barked out commands like an army sergeant training raw recruits. But an undertone of excitement and happiness cushioned them as they fell on our ears.

My brother, Gilly, and I tripped and skipped after Father as he harnessed the horses to the wagon. Our baby sister, Francisca, at eight months old, was, of course, far too small to join our adventure. The big horses stomped and snorted cottony puffs of fog from their huge nostrils. I was nine years old—almost grown up. My body was stretching out, becoming long-limbed and slim. My dark hair was losing its fine, baby gloss and becoming thick and long. This Christmas Eve, Mama and Father would allow me to help light the candles on our Tannenbaum.

Trekking up into the hills to bring back the finest tree for Christmas was a ritual made possible by our friends, the Schultz family. It was good for a farmer to have a nice big woodlot, and theirs was one of the most beautiful in the Schwarzwald. In summer, it was blessed by the trills of singing birds, the dazzle of butterfly wings, and the rippling hum of crystal water flowing down from the mountains to the west. In all seasons, the woodlot was thick with silver fir, beech, and alder. In winter, snow cushioned the wagon's runners and silenced all sounds but the sweet notes of winter birds. We trundled aboard the wagon, and the search was on!

Father did not consider Christmas complete without a tree. He loved the rituals of the season—the scents of Mama's holiday treats baking in the woodstove, the Advent wreath of pinecones and holly berries. Best of all was the magical Christmas pyramid, made of light ash strips, delicately arranged so that the pyramid rotated when the heat from lighted candles on the first tier turned the paddle wheel perched on top, coaxing the little angels it carried to turn graceful circles.

When we reached the stand of trees with the thickest, most fragrant firs, Father set the brake, and we all hopped off. Gilly squealed as he landed in the thigh-high snow. He grabbed the stem of the nearest fir, a spindly sprout just barely taller than he was. "Look at this one!" he called, his high, soprano voice breaking the stillness of the forest. Father and I laughed. I suppose the scrubby little thing looked big through little Gilly's five-year-old eyes. He was thin and small for his age, but spritely and full of life. He had mischievous gray-blue eyes, the color of clouds reflected in water, and dark blond hair, the kind that turns brown with the years.

"This one is perfect! It's straight as an arrow," I called from deeper in the forest. For a few minutes, no one answered, and I was alone, surrounded by trees. I felt my heart grow big as I took in the winter forest. The sharp air invigorated my whole body. The thick tree trunks stood straight as sentinels on guard duty. The evergreen branches closed above me like the soaring apse of the church. *This is where my soul lives*, I thought.

Father's whistle drew me back to our quest. Gilly and I came plowing through the waves of white as fast as we could. We knew the moment we saw Father gazing up through the branches of the silver fir that his choice would be the best Christmas tree ever—thick and straight, as beautiful a tree as had ever grown.

Gilly and I used the trees as cover as we assaulted each other with snowballs while Father sawed away at the trunk. When the stately fir fell, the pillow of snow cushioned its fall, so not a single branch was broken. We laughed as we struggled to load the thick fir onto the wagon. Father posted Gilly at the tip, while I positioned myself close to midway down the trunk. Father, of course, benefitted little from our efforts to help him load the tree into the wagon, but Gilly and I felt like hardy woodsmen helping him win the tussle with the fir. On the trip home, we bellowed out "The Happy Wanderer"—"I love to go a-wandering along the mountain track"—singing loudly if not well, as the big, sure-footed Belgians plodded down the hill, descending into the gathering darkness. Our voices rose into the crystal night as stars slowly poked their sparkling faces through the midnight-blue fabric of the night sky.

A few weeks earlier, the night before St. Nicholas's Day, Gilly and I had cleaned and polished our shoes and placed them by the hearth. Little Francisca did not yet wear shoes, so she once again missed the excitement. Gilly and I had awoken the next morning, expecting to see our shoes filled with walnuts, chocolates, or, rarest of all, an orange. Instead, we'd found them empty. Gilly still believed that the old Saint Nicholas snuck in through the door on his saint's day to bestow these riches while we slept. I, of course, knew better. But it did not make me feel better knowing that it was Mama who had neglected to fill our shoes with the expected goodies. My heart fell, and my throat constricted. But I quickly swallowed my disappointment when I saw Gilly's sad expression. His face crumpled, squeezing tears from the corners of his eyes.

"Have I been a bad boy? Is that why St. Nicholas didn't come to our house?" He struggled not to let the tears fall.

"No, no, *liebchen*, you're a good boy! St. Nicholas must have been so busy that he didn't have time to visit every house. Maybe he needs more than one night to make his visits. After all, just think of all the children in our town, and there are so many towns! We must be patient and give him another chance." Swallowing my own disappointment, I did my best to console my little brother.

I reported the tragedy to Father. He tucked a few pfennigs into my hand.

"You're a smart girl. I know you can make your brother happy," he said calmly and sent me out the door to the market.

I felt proud of my responsibility but worried that I might not find what

I wanted. On December 7, the day after the saint's day, the market was picked over. I searched from one stall to the next, my hopes growing dim. It took nearly two hours, but I discovered a few hidden treasures among the leftovers—some sugared almonds, crystalized honey candies, plums, and spiced cookie bars, slightly stale but still sweet. There were no oranges, but I managed to hunt down some black and red currants and two good, tart apples. These would do. That night, St. Nicholas managed to find our house. Although Gilly smiled, a little sadness hid in the corner of his heart.

I was angry. How could Mama have forgotten us this way! This was just the most recent of her sins of omission. She forgot her housework too. We sometimes had to wear dirty socks, stiffened from drying near the woodstove when she did not finish the laundry. Last summer, we'd had an invasion of ants because she hadn't mopped up sugar from the floor after making kuchen. I wondered if she would confess her neglect to our old parish pastor, Father Dinny, when she made her next confession. This was not the first time I'd had to step up and take on a responsibility that should have been hers. Mama had become lethargic, sleeping day and night, neglecting her chores, rarely smiling, and never singing as she worked, the way she used to do.

Two years prior, a few days after Christmas, when I was seven and Gilly was three, our sister Genoveva had arrived. Genoveva was so beautiful when she was born. She was fat and healthy, with lively, alert eyes, though she had an unfortunate baldness. Mama told me this was typical for blond babies and her hair would grow soon enough. With my dark brown mop of hair, I'd never had that problem.

I remember Genoveva's birth well. It was two years before, 1803, only four days after we'd all enjoyed a very happy Christmas. Winter weather that year had been unusually harsh. Frau Kopf, the midwife, struggled through the snow-clotted streets, barely arriving in time to boil the water and banish Gilly and me to our room. "Get to your room, and don't come out until I call you!" Frau Kopf's voice seemed frantic.

"And you, Herr Burkart, go to the tavern and have a beer! Your dear wife, Maria Anna, does not need you now that I'm here."

"Has Mama turned into a wolf?" Gilly wondered with dread as his imagination, fed on a diet of dark folktales, translated Mama's howls.

"No, I think Mama needs to howl to help make the baby come; otherwise, it will be stuck inside her belly forever." I wasn't sure I believed this, but I had no better explanation.

Gilly and I cowered on our beds for what seemed like hours. Finally, the deep howling stopped, and a shrill, high-pitched voice replaced it.

"Anastasia, put on your boots and go get your father. Tell him it's a girl!" Frau Kopf, now disheveled in her blood-soaked apron, demanded.

I climbed into my winter boots. My unfastened coat flapped around my knees as I ran through the snow to the tavern. Father bolted from his seat at the old oak bar, not waiting for me to catch up. I could barely keep sight of him as we ran through the darkened streets.

The winter Genoveva was born continued to be brutal. Snow came early and deep. Some days my classroom was half-empty. The children who lived too far away stayed home. Those students who were able to trek through the deep snow sniffled their way through their lessons. Our whole family suffered fevers and coughs. By the time disaster struck in February, we were all thoroughly tired of winter.

"Anastasia, bring in more firewood." Mama's voice was edged with fear. She was normally a mild-mannered, indulgent mother. My heart jolted in surprise. I was only seven years old, and bringing the wood in was a difficult task.

"That's a good girl. Now, can you go get …" Her voice trailed off. The sound of Genoveva's coughing interrupted us.

It was hard to believe the rasping sound that wracked her little body came from such a tiny baby. Mama held our beautiful, bald baby over a pot of boiling water, a blanket draped over both their heads as they inhaled the vapor. The apothecary had given Mama a pine-scented jelly to rub on Genoveva's chest and belly. For a while, it seemed to help. But the coughing interrupted our conversations more and more often. Eventually, our baby lost interest in eating. Mama tried to tempt her to nurse, but she turned her head away.

By January, her cough seemed less vigorous. By early February, she lay limp in Mama's arms. Her little cheeks, so fat two months ago, were now red, but not in a healthy, rosy way. Her blue eyes seemed larger than before. They shone with an unnatural glassy sheen. Finally, we wished she would cough again rather than struggle for breath with tortured, choking, gurgling gasps.

By late February, Genoveva lay silent. The tiny body of our Christmas angel collapsed in on itself, like a rag doll that lost its stuffing. Her pine coffin was so small it could have been meant for a child's doll. Mama stopped talking. She went to bed and turned her face to the wall. She stayed there day and night, rising only to perform her most basic duties. She looked at Father, Gilly, and me with vacant eyes, not appearing to see us at all.

Mama lived almost completely in her small universe of pain. At first, I missed her. There were no more giggles when I spilled the flour while helping her make strudel in our cozy kitchen. I no longer felt the comfort and security of her companionship. The happy, warmhearted Mama I knew had been devoured by melancholy. Poor Gilly had suffered most from Mama's distance over the past two years. When he climbed into her bed to snuggle or tried to get her to sing him a song or tell him a story, Mama did not respond. I became little Gilly's lifeline and best friend, taking the place in his heart that Mama left unfilled.

I was growing up fast and tried to help Father and Gilly in every way I could. Though my efforts were clumsy and unskilled, Father never criticized my attempts at cooking and cleaning. But after a few months, he hired Frau Belcher to help us.

Despite eating only sporadically, Mama's belly grew fat, while her face seemed to collapse in on itself. I should have realized what was happening but was unprepared when Francisca arrived in April. Francisca was long like a sausage. She seldom cried and had a somber face for an infant. She seldom smiled and gazed at Mama with serious eyes. With her thick mat of dark hair sticking straight out from her little head, she looked nothing like Genoveva. But Mama wanted to use Genoveva's name for this child too.

"No!" Father rejected the idea emphatically. "This child will have her own name. Every baby needs a name of its own." He put his foot down and would not be swayed.

"But look at my family. All of us have the same name—Maria Rosina, Maria Francisca, and myself, Maria Anna," Mama argued.

"Yes, that's exactly my point! I can hardly keep them straight. No one calls them by their baptismal names in any case. They all use their second names. Why have a name if you are not going to use it?"

"But I haven't chosen another name. I was afraid to." Mama bowed her head, and the shadow of grief passed over her.

She did her best to make her arguments, but Father was not persuaded.

"Dear Anna, I understand. But, no, we are not using our dead baby's name. What is your favorite sister's name?" Father's tone was soft and compassionate.

Mother brightened a bit. "It's Francisca. We grew up so close, almost like twins."

"Okay then. Francisca it is!" Father was triumphant.

Mama reached out for Father's hand. Father cupped her small hand in both of his. They were still for several moments.

Francisca devoured Mama's attention. It seemed whatever small reserves of energy Mama had were devoted to keeping Francisca's body and soul together. She was still my Mama, but she was not the same. Her eyes were less lively; she laughed less often. She sometimes sat and stared into the distance. We did not disturb her.

This Christmas, though, I was nine, and Gilly was five. It had been eight months since Francisca's birth and two years since we'd lost our precious Genoveva. Gilly was only three when she died and didn't remember at all. He never knew the lively, happy mother I had known. Mama made an effort to be festive. She wore her finest dress and curled the ringlets that hung over her ears. Though we appreciated her improved mood, we could not completely erase the scars of neglect.

Two days before Christmas, little Gilly and I visited the Christmas market in the center of town. Though I had done the marketing for the family often this year and was familiar with the abundance the vendors' stands held, the Christmas market was something entirely different. The air had smelled like impending snow for more than a week, but that night, the gray sky held onto its flakes. The evening chill only added to the festive holiday atmosphere. Torches blazed. The smells of plum cider and gingerbread cookies were like delightful, vaporous streams in which we swam. The very best of the season's sausages hung fat and juicy from the butcher's stall. The sights and smells competed for our attention with the jugglers and puppeteers. The Swiss-German band dressed in their festive lederhosen enlivened the holiday atmosphere. Gilly paused in front of the puppeteer's little stage. A long-nosed Kasperle puppet character pummeled the unfortunate tax collector, while his sister, Gretel, kicked the bad man in the shins. The adults laughed and clapped along with the children, booing the villains and cheering the naughty Kasperle. Gilly stared, entranced by the farcical spectacle.

"Come on, Gilly. Don't just stand there. We have something to do!" I demanded, as I grabbed his hand. Though he let himself be dragged away, his eyes did not leave the puppet stage until it was out of sight.

We were two children on a mission. I had saved enough money to surprise Father and Mama. We needed to find one special item to add to the Christmas tree. It delighted me to imagine their surprised smiles. This would be the first year we gave them a Christmas gift. We held tightly to each other's hands as we threaded our way through the wonderful confections and colorful handicrafts. We bumped into big bellies, stepped on toes, and narrowly escaped being knocked about like bowling pins in the crowd.

Gilly broke from my grip and disappeared into the crowd. His squeal convinced me he had been mortally wounded. I hustled to catch sight of him. All I could see of my impish brother was the top of his little head, bouncing through the sea of woolen coats. When I finally caught up to him, I stopped short, my scolding words swallowed like a gulp of spiced cider.

"There it is!" he cried.

And there it was, the perfect gift, lying among dozens of baubles on the glassmaker's table—a beautiful glass star painted a translucent gold, its surface reflecting light from every direction. Out from under my apron came my little drawstring purse. I counted out my pfennigs, my life savings, and plunked them down on the table.

"And where did a skinny, little fraulein like you get so much money?" asked the glass vendor.

I stretched as tall as I could, threw my shoulders back, and blurted out, "I work for the *schneider*'s guild." It was a bit of an exaggeration, but Father had started to pay me to run errands for his guild. He need not have paid me, as most of the other fathers did not pay their children for errands. But Father said he was trying to teach me the value of money so I would not squander it.

8

The glassmaker's puffy face, ruddy from the chill, became ruddier as he grumbled something about these "modern" ideas of paying children, much less paying a girl! I shrugged off his disapproval, snatched the beautiful golden star, and silently blessed my father for his "modern" ideas.

Actually, Father's modern ideas were not his alone. One evening, a few months ago, Father had invited a few of his friends, other guild craftsmen, into our home for an evening of fine fall Märzen beer and a game of *schafkopf.* The card game was always lively and often generated a great deal of shouting, bantering, and laughing. I was confined to the little bedroom I shared with Gilly; our presence was not welcome, and we were instructed not to show our faces. But that did not prevent me from peeking through the crack I left open. The air was thick with the smell of malty beer and hardworking men. Knuckles rapped the table as the players took tricks. Enthusiasm grew more boisterous as more rounds of beer were poured. Later in the evening, the jovial conversation mellowed as the men leaned back in their chairs and lit their pipes. Gilly hated the smell, but it comforted and calmed me.

France was a topic of urgent interest in our town. Gruntal still showed the scars of Napoleon's last conflict that had ended a few years before I was born. Though we had struck a bargain with Napoleon, our fragile peace had a price. He treated us as vassals. Now Napoleon was again flexing his muscle, annexing German-speaking territories west of the Rhine, shutting down monasteries, and confiscating Catholic Church property. Our town was mostly Catholic, so his policies were hotly resented. Even so, some of the ideas of the French Revolution seeped into the men's conversation.

"Everyone has the power of reason," argued Herr Greiser, the miller. "Therefore everyone should be able to think for himself." When I was little, I believed the flour permeating the mill caused his pasty white complexion and yellow hair.

"That's nonsense. The ignorant cannot reason as the educated man can. The ignorant are ruled by unreason, superstition, and blind obedience," growled Herr Krueger. As a clock maker, he was one of the wealthier burghers. His views did not surprise me, as all his children terrified their schoolmates with tales of the tyrannical way he ruled his family.

"Yes, it is true the uneducated are more superstitious, but we all believe in the mysteries of our faith, don't we?" put in Herr Stein, known by all as Peter the Pious.

"That's different! Those mysteries were given to us by God, as were our powers of reason. All humans possess the ability to be enlightened, and humanity is progressing toward more maturity in its understanding." Father spoke these words that seemed to me the wisest so far.

"Who do you mean by 'all people'? Surely you don't include your women! Women need the guidance and rule of a man," huffed Herr Kopf.

"Ha, ha, ha! So says the man whose wife brings as much prosperity to your household with her midwifery as you do as a cooper. Where would you be without her? Do you think she needs to be ruled by you?" Herr Kleinmann's laugh sounded more like an accusation than a joke. His sense of humor often became sharp and pointed after his second or third stein.

"All right now, friends, this will never be settled tonight. Let's part friends and brothers. We all know our women share as much ability to reason as we do. Though I must admit, their reason does fail them at times." He smiled good-naturedly. Was Father talking about Mama? It was certainly true that Mama sometimes seemed beyond the reach of reason. With the geniality of the evening thus preserved, the get-together ended amid much back slapping and foot stomping out the door.

I was sure the future would be different for me than the world Mama had grown up in, confined as she was to hearth and children. I could understand why Father had chosen her. Maria Anna Stehl had been courted by many suitors. She was a handsome woman. Soft, wavy, brown hair framed her oval face. Her gray eyes were clear and intelligent. There was a softness around her edges. She seemed fragile, a bit uncertain of herself, subdued, and reluctant to assert her opinion. I would be different! I would be strong and smart and would have the opportunity to be an independent woman! Of course, neither Father nor the others were speaking of equality for women exactly, but I didn't see why those glorious principles should not apply to me. After all, Father already encouraged my industriousness by paying me a few pefennigs for running errands.

When Christmas Eve finally arrived, we dragged the tree up the stairs to the parlor.

"Look, look, Mama." Gilly desperately tried to get Mama's approval as he drew her attention the beautiful Christmas Tannenbaum.

"It's lovely, Gilly. Did you help choose it?" Mama's voice was kindly and indulgent but sounded detached.

"I saw it first!" Gilly beamed with pride, as though he thought what he said was really true. Which, of course, it wasn't. Father had seen the tree first.

Father and I smiled at each other like conspirators and let Gilly take the credit.

The Christmas tree took up the entire center of the parlor. It filled the whole house with forest smells. We inhaled the joy of the season, along with the scent of the tree. Gilly danced around the tree like a forest gnome. Baby Francisca squealed.

Mama, Father, Gilly, and I draped our tree with ribbons, small shapes made from dried dough, Mama's beautiful tatted lace snowflakes, and winter birds. The winter birds were my favorites. Made from Mama's clothespins and rooster feathers, they told the story of the night in ages past when a flock of birds escaped certain death in a terrible winter storm by sheltering in the embrace of a dense fir tree. In return, the birds gave the tree their blessing so it would always be green and known as the symbol of everlasting life, even in the dead of winter. Now the tree was passing the blessing on to us. We worked silently but with full hearts.

After the decorations were in place, I secured the candles to the ends of the lower branches so they would not tip over or drip on the floor as Father expertly attached them to the upper branches. We stood back and enjoyed the grace and beauty of our creation, fine-tuning the placement of each ornament. Finally, Mama snuggled the crèche into a bed of fir boughs under the tree.

Mama gave Francisca an ornament to place on the bottom branch. All things that Francisca grasped went directly into her voracious little mouth. Mama had to pry the bauble out of her pudgy hand until she let go. Francisca wailed, and Mama laughed. My head turned sharply, involuntarily toward her. Mama's laugh had startled me. I had not heard her laugh for the longest time!

My dear father handed me a long fire stick, and I lit the candles on the lower branches as he carefully leaned over my head to reach the upper branches. The tree was magnificent! Christmas felt right, almost right enough to make our family feel whole.

I offered up a little prayer of hope that the loving Mama I knew had returned to us. Two years ago, Mama had withdrawn into a universe of distraction. Gilly and I could hardly ever reach her there. Today, her laughter showered down on us like a blessing from heaven.

She smiled at Gilly and me, each of us in turn, and then disappeared. She returned with a basket covered with an old, knitted towel. Her hand fumbled under the towel, and when she withdrew it, she had a Marzipan cookie dipped in Swiss chocolate. She handed it to Francisca. The moment the baby's tongue touched the treat, her eyes lit up, and her four little teeth started gnawing away with intense concentration. She would never be the same after her first taste of sweetness.

"Where's my cookie?" Gilly insisted.

"Calm down, Gilly. You will get your turn." Mama chided, the hint of a smile playing at the corners of her mouth.

Gilly could hardly contain himself. He squealed and bounced on one foot and then the other. Out of the basket came a carved, wooden puppet mounted on a long stick. It was both scary and funny with its long nose, mischievous eyes, and toothy grin.

"This puppet is called Kasperle." Father explained.

"I know who Kasperle is! I've seen him at the puppet show in the market. He can beat the devils away. He bonks them with his stick. He's funny and plays tricks on people." Gilly picked up Mama's wooden spoon and ran around the room, banging on everything within reach, attempting to imitate Kasperle.

"We have something for you too, Anastasia. We want to thank you for being such a big help." Mama pulled the towel aside, and inside the basket lay a dress.

I looked at Mama and then at Father. My heart couldn't decide if it belonged in my throat or my toes. The room went from a normal, cool wintery comfort to a torrid summer sultriness as my face reddened.

"Go ahead. Pick it up. It's for you." Father said, gently prodding me out of my paralyzed amazement.

I lifted the dress by its shoulders and pressed it up against my body. I had never owned such a dress. Father was a tailor, the master schneider of our town, known throughout the community as honest, hardworking, and fair. The dress was a masterwork of his skill. The sleeves were slightly puffy at the top, tapering to a tight fit around the wrists. The waist was encircled by a bright red ribbon. But the collar! The collar was lace made by the finest tatter in Gruntal, my own mama. She hadn't forgotten me after all in her melancholia.

"There's one more thing," Mama interrupted my thoughts. I reluctantly put the dress aside.

"More?" I was incredulous.

Mama pulled the last surprise from her basket and handed it to me. It was a small, exquisite book, leather bound, with grapevines and leaves painted around the outside border. It had thick ivory pages with ragged edges. Fascinated, I opened the first page.

"Mama, I don't understand. There is nothing written in this book." My puzzlement was complete.

"I know." Her slight smile seemed directed inward, at herself, not me. "Your heart needs a place to rest its troubles. This is a book of days. In it, you can write all your thoughts and feelings. It will be yours, and only yours, forever."

"But what will I write?" I was still mystified.

"Write what you see, what you think, what you feel. Write your joys and troubles. Write for yourself alone. You will see. This book will become your best friend if you let it."

"Thank you, Mama. I don't know what to say."

"No need to say anything. In time, you will understand."

I set the book aside. But first things first. "Gilly, go get our box. Go!"

Off he ran, dove under the bed, and returned with a small packet encased in bright paper. He proudly handed it to Father. "It's for both of you," he said, bursting with pride.

Father and Mama drew together, huddling over it. Gilly clutched my hand. They looked at it and then each other. The gold-painted, glass star!

"Go ahead, put it up. It's for the top of the tree." Gilly squealed. "It points the way to heaven."

We stood around our beautiful, blazing tree. Father began the lovely incantation of *"Stille nacht, heilege nacht."* We joined hands and sang the beautiful hymn together. Even baby Francisca, who was chocolate from elbow to ear, tried to join in, bubbling and cooing.

Christmas Day dawned frosty. Ice crystals sparkled on every surface. Hoarfrost gilded every fallen leaf and turned the branches of every tree into magic wands. Even the air glistened. This lovely Christmas Day, I wore my beautiful new dress. If a dress can transform you into a better, more elegant person, then my dress certainly possessed that magic. By the time the sun set, the morning's crystals had turned into big, fat flakes to match our big, fat bellies, stuffed with Christmas treats.

That night was the first time I tried to translate my heart onto the pages of my book of days, Mama's gift.

CHAPTER 2

THE SCHOOLGIRL

1808

Fasnacht was in February in this, my twelfth year. The pre-Lenten Fasnacht parade was my favorite of our many festivals. Men and women dressed up in flamboyant costumes of every imaginable description, as priests, nobles, or ancient folktale characters. Under the cover of masks and costumes, perhaps further emboldened by the courage of wine, beer, and brandy, even staid citizens reveled in pushing the limits of good behavior. Witches cackled and shook their brooms. Townspeople wearing elaborate, frightening wooden masks howled outrageously to drive out the evil spirits that had settled in the town over the cold, dreary winter. Once the spirits had been scared away, warmer weather and healthy crops would surely soon appear. The ancient folks who'd made this valley home many centuries ago had celebrated this ceremony long before our church ever existed. They had also donned masks and lit bonfires to chase away winter and coax the gods into blessing them with a bountiful growing season. We were their heirs, and their spirit still lived in us.

Crusty, late-season snow still clung to the hills, but I stayed warm. Father had transformed me from a twelve-year-old girl into a bear, swaddled in a costume of warm French terrycloth, brown and fuzzy from head to toe. A hood enshrouded my face. Mama had even fashioned a black nose for me from an oversize thimble Father had gotten as a sample from a traveling vendor, and she smeared black circles around my eyes with ash from the fireplace. I ran through the crowd roaring and threatening all who came near me.

Herr Kleinmann tottered down the street with his stein full.

"Be careful there, Herr Kleinmann," warned Herr Kohler, costumed as a loaf of golden bread, after Herr Kleinmann nearly lost his balance and bounced off the soft, human bread loaf.

"I'm just getting my fill before lent dries up this miserly town," Herr Kleinmann growled back. He was not alone in his overindulgence. He was not the only man staggering through the crowded streets.

This year, Rupert Schultz was dressed up as old Father Dinny. Father Dinny was the iron fist that governed every one of the school's children, and his entrance into the classroom prompted all the students to pop out of their seats and sing in unison, "Guten Tag, Father Dinny." Rupert was the oldest of the five Schultz children and my favorite. He was a funny, blond-haired dynamo, with big blue eyes that dominated his face and a comical, crooked smile that never ceased to charm me. For Fasnacht this year, he'd fattened his stomach with pillows in imitation of the portly priest and wrapped a clerical robe he'd pilfered from the sacristy around him. He pretended to terrorize the children, berating their poor marks in school and threatening them with punishment for their bad behavior.

"And you!" Rupert chased down a poor boy from the third class. "You have been shooting peas through chamomile stems, terrorizing the little girls!" Rupert bellowed.

The little boy cowered momentarily before he recognized Rupert and then tried to run away.

"You stay right here," Rupert ordered, catching the boy by the collar before he could flee.

"That will be four Our Fathers and three Hail Marys for you!" Rupert prescribed the boy his penance for the infraction.

Everyone within earshot laughed loudly as the red-faced victim finally escaped.

Rupert seemed to know the transgressions of every child in town. All the children and many of the adults who had experienced Father Dinny's despotism laughed heartily.

After the frivolity of Fasnacht, we all settled into our sober Lenten routine, fasting, doing penance for our sins, and meditating on the sufferings of Jesus and how he died for us. I accepted these somber teachings but struggled to examine my conscience, searching for the many sins I had supposedly committed.

The season of penance passed, and a beautiful spring erupted from the sooty, gray snowbanks. Plum blossoms filled the air with perfume. The lemony sun encouraged the lilies of the valley to add their sweet scents to the fragrant breezes.

On this morning in June, I flew down the stairs and out the door, snatching the strap of my book bag, worried I would miss meeting Katy and Matilda at our spot on the corner in front of the baker's shop.

"Goodbye, Mama. I'll see you this afternoon."

Mama, standing at the sink washing the morning's dishes, grunted absentmindedly but did not lift her head to bid me goodbye.

Though I was late, my two best friends were there waiting for me, chattering and fidgeting. The irrepressible energy of new awakening burst out everywhere—from the budding trees, from the river surging with melted mountain snow, and from three girls on the threshold of womanhood. We linked arms and skipped down the street to the schoolroom, lighthearted, with no concerns more serious than worrying whether our final marks would be high enough to please our parents.

We girls considered ourselves the best and the brightest our town had to offer. Katy Herr, Matilda Kohler, and I had been fast friends for years, since the age of six, when we were the youngest in our room of girl students. I could depend on at least one of them to join me at our skating pond above Greiser's mill or at the many festivals our town celebrated. I was the best student, but my hazel eyes; slim body; and straight, nearly black hair were quite unremarkable. Katy, with her long, flaxen waves and blue eyes, was the prettiest. And Matilda, whose family ran the bakery where we met to walk to school, had an appealing roundness to her face, with ruddy cheeks and dancing eyes. With her impish good humor, she could make us laugh any time she chose. Every day before the school bell rang, I ran down the hill to meet my friends. Katy ran up from the lower town. And Matilda simply stepped out her front door.

Unlike most of the houses in our town that butted up against each other like peas in a pod, the bakery was freestanding and did not share walls with an adjoining house. It was unusual in other ways too. Like most of the other houses, its exterior walls were framed with substantial hand-hewn oak logs. The log framework and the angled corner braces created a thick, woody skeleton that could be seen on the outside as well as the inside. But Herr Kohler, the baker, had plastered over the outside of the first level, creating a smooth exterior surface. He'd then enlisted the town's best artist to create a tempting tableau of round loaves of bread, plum tortes, apple strudels, and jelly-filled *pfannkuchen* doughnuts on the smooth exterior. The intoxicating aroma of the bakery, together with the mouthwatering artistry, made it impossible to pass by without pushing the door open to see what delights awaited inside.

By contrast, the building that housed Katy's father's shoemaker shop and living quarters was simple. It was also the newest home, built on a vacated lot. The previous owner had disassembled his posts and beams, carefully numbering them like the pieces of a puzzle. Then he'd loaded them on a huge wagon and hauled them off to Offenburg, where he'd reassembled them. The old beams were his personal property. Like one's furniture, they were too valuable to leave behind. He'd hauled away the crumbling wattle and daub that had filled the spaces between the beams, leaving a rare vacant lot in the lower side of town. With the sides of the adjoining houses exposed, you could see the variety of materials used to fill in the walls between the timbers—mortar, hardened mud, and sticks woven together and cemented in with clay. Katy's father's new structure used the traditional hewn log framework, but he chose red bricks arranged in a chevron pattern between the timbers. It provided a refreshing new look standing amid the traditional half-timbered buildings.

My family's ancient house, near the upper edge of town, lay at the base of the darkly wooded hills. Our house was old, and not quite straight, tilting a bit to one side, but it embodied the spirit of our town, Gruntal. It was an ancient building, but it was beautiful in my eyes. Our living quarters were on the second story over the street-level tailor shop. The upper story cantilevered precariously out over the narrow street. Some long-forgotten master carpenter had exquisitely carved the wooden angle bracings below the protruding edge into beautiful filigreed scrollwork. I never tired of studying the faces of the gargoyles, wild animals, and angels or the intricately carved grapevines like those that still thrived in our beautiful valley. At this time of year, all the town's hausfrauen vied to create the most beautiful window boxes, which overflowed with colorful blooms. The flowers were a symbol of our cheerful optimism and civic pride.

The bakery where my friends and I met was nestled in the center of town, just two blocks below St. Michael's Church. The plain limestone church, sparingly adorned with four arched windows, loomed over us. One round window above the carved double doors glowered down on us like the judgmental eye of God. Despite its somber look, St. Michael's was the heart and soul of our devoutly Catholic town and the gathering place for Sunday Mass, holy days, church picnics, social and religious meetings, weddings, funerals, and baptisms. The church records held the entire history of our little town. A small stone building abutting the church sheltered our little school. Our school building mirrored the church's stony severity, but for the past six years, the small classroom had been my refuge and the focal point of our lives.

Katy, Matilda, and I attended class with some of the other burghers' daughters in a classroom adjoining that of the boys. We could hear the boys' meister ranting and slapping the table, and sometimes the boys, when their grasp of Latin conjugations proved lacking, with his ash pointer. Luckily, we girls did not need to learn Latin but stuck to our curriculum of reading, writing, arithmetic, and religion. In school, I was free of my complicated, confusing feelings about my mama. In school, I was free to think and learn. I read everything I could find and improved my math skills as best I could. I was convinced it would help me become the independent woman I wanted to be. Besides, I wanted Father to be proud.

The one thing at which all three of us girls excelled was giggling. Anything could set us off—an accidental burp, a boy with mismatched stockings, a hausfrau with unruly hair protruding peculiarly from her head scarf. When we were together, these things were unaccountably hilarious. There were times we laughed so hard tears squeezed from our eyes, and we nearly suffocated, unable to catch our breath. We knew each other so well we could communicate with sidelong glances or smirks. More than once, one or the other of us was rapped on the knuckles by Sister Gregory's stout ruler for winking at each other in class, sharing some joke only we understood. But we didn't mind. The occasional red knuckle was a small price to pay for our friendship.

The school year ended, and we girls returned to our families. Summer is a deceptive season; the air lays peacefully on the hills caressing the tender leaves, and time seems to stand still. The world hangs suspended between the purity of the azure blue sky and the earthy fecundity below. Whenever I could, I stole away to walk the maze of trails that threaded through the high hills above the town. I loved hiking up hills, planting one foot in front of the other in a determined march up to the high places. I loved the way my uphill march made my heart beat harder and my breath quicken. It heightened my senses and made me feel more alive, more a part of the world around me. I would lay down on the soft carpet of pine needles and close my eyes. I indulged my senses in smells of summer—the loamy richness of the earth, ripening berries, the ineffable scent of green leaves, and the tangy richness of pines.

But time did not stand still, and soon the long days shortened into fall. Brisk winds blew away the summer leaves. And before long, another year was drawing to a close.

Rupert's family and mine had been friends forever. It was their woodlot that supplied our Christmas tree each year. Rupert and I both sang in the children's choir at our stern-looking stone church, with its imposing tower, venerable pipe organ, and dark choir loft. Gruntal took an unseemly pride in its children's choir. The high, pure voices of young singers reminded the people of angels singing at the foot of God's throne. The highlight of each Christmas Eve was midnight Mass. Nothing could be more inspirational than seeing the apse of old St. Michael's Kirche, with its off-center spire, transformed from a stone-cold, black cavern into a warm grotto, awash in the amber glow of handheld candles.

This year, as we always did, parishioners ambled through the cobbled streets, hands plunged deeply into our pockets, smiling and greeting each other. Like pilgrims flocking to a holy site of miracles, we were drawn to the stone church as if it exerted a gravitational pull. We broke from the throng entering the church and made our way up the narrow, winding stairs to the choir loft, where the old church seemed darkest and coldest. Our warm winter coats brushed against each other. Our feet shuffled in silence. We choristers took our position as singers seriously. Musical ability was valued almost as much as athletic ability or academic success. We learned the Latin Masses, Gregorian chants, and German hymns as perfectly as we could. The soft, dreamy look on Sister Alma's face and the sound of soft sighs from below were ample reward for our efforts. I loved looking down on the sea of parishioners from the choir loft. Their humid, woolen coats and hats exuded a comforting earthy tang that wafted up to us.

"Will you go skating again this year?" Rupert whispered as we ascended the spiral stairs that disappeared into the dark tower.

"Yes, of course." I giggled, remembering the wild fun we had last year.

I couldn't wait to go skating again. Playing Red Rover and Crack the Whip and careening into the encircling snowbanks warmed my blood so much I hardly noticed the icy air.

"Well, then, I will see you at the pond when the ice is good and hard." Rupert's elbow shot out and speared me in the ribs.

My eyes shot daggers at him. Rupert just grinned his crooked grin. I could not be angry.

Sister Alma chose the child choristers for the purity of their voices, their ability to memorize, and their reliably good behavior. Our high, sweet voices echoed off the old stone walls, sounding ethereal as they floated over the worshipers. The chords of the sacred music rained down on the people below like blessings from God. The last thing the serious but sweet Sister Alma needed was a rowdy crew of school-age children distracting the worshipers from the solemnity of Mass. No boys whose voices were starting to change were allowed to sing. This year, Rupert was fourteen, two years older than I, and his days in the choir were almost over. His voice was no longer childishly pure and high. He still sang in a mellow alto register, but the cracks and squeaks that signaled puberty were beginning to embarrass him.

Now that we were twelve, we girls had begun to bend our heads together, tittering about this boy or that boy. Boys who had been invisible to us just a year before now held some fascination. We assessed their good and bad traits, picking out our favorites, gossiping and laughing. I shared this girlish pleasure, but I did not want them giggling about Rupert in that way. I blushed when they described his wavy, blond hair; cornflower blue eyes; and charming, off center smile. Hearing the name of my childhood friend and neighbor summoned a sort of sinking feeling, a feeling I had never before experienced. It was neither sadness nor joy but a titillating fascination. Rupert and I were friends, as we had always been, yet not quite friends. My feelings for Rupert left my face flushed and my mind confused. I was inexplicably eager to run into him on the streets or in the market but also felt uncharacteristically shy and a little silly when I did.

One lovely, winter, quarter moon night, my girlfriends and I looped lazy circles around the pond. Gliding effortlessly arm in arm, we were more interested in gossiping than in playing Crack the Whip and rolling in snow-banks. It was getting late. My friends left me and headed to the warming hut to remove the blades strapped to their boots and walk home. I skated a few more loops, hands clasped pensively behind my back. My long strides sounded like knives scratching the icy surface. The air had that special, in-describable midwinter quality, biting as it rolls over the tongue but leaving you thirsty for more. I filled my lungs, wondering how the cold air could be without scent of any kind, yet full of the essence of winter.

As I pondered this mystery, Rupert glided past me. He slowed, and his hand grazed mine as he passed by a little more closely than was usual. A jolt passed through me as though I had suddenly fallen through a hole in the ice. Was it accidental? I looked around. No one else seemed to notice. I coasted to the warming hut and loosened the laces on my skates. Suddenly Rupert appeared next to me.

"Can I untie those laces for you?" he asked, kneeling before me.

Flustered, I couldn't respond. Without a word, Rupert untied the leather thongs that tied my battered, double-bladed skates to my boots. I knotted them together to form a long lanyard of laces that I draped over my shoulder and began my walk home.

It was a windless, half moon night, very cold and dark. I inhaled in small gulps so the freezing air would not sting my lungs and exhaled dense puffs of vapor. The packed snow crunched and squeaked beneath my boots. I walked, staring straight up at the crystalline sky. Like the milkman's old horse, I knew every step of the way home without looking, so I was surprised when I bumped straight into someone.

"Oh, I'm so sorry. I wasn't looking where I was going," I blustered.

"It's my fault. You weren't expecting to see me here." I heard Rupert's familiar voice before I recognized his form emerge from the glistening night.

"Is that you, Rupert? What are you doing here? Your house is …" I pointed vaguely toward the bare grapevines on the hill above us.

He stopped me, took my right hand, drew me to him, and leaned in. I felt like the Indian cobras I had seen in a book, mesmerized before the swami's flute. For the briefest moment, our lips touched. I did not deliberately pull away. I was so startled that my skates slipped off my shoulder and clattered to the frozen street. Before I could catch my breath, he was gone, running in the opposite direction toward his own warm home as I bent to pick up my skates.

I was confused. What would my friends think if they had seen us? Their hilarious laughter would have been mortifying. Hot tears sprang to my eyes just thinking of what their reaction would have been. What would my father think? He would lecture me sternly and march off to have a little chat with Herr Schultz. Who knew what my inscrutable mama would have thought? She might have shaken her finger in my face and assigned me extra chores. But she might just as easily have relaxed her shoulders, tilted her head to one side, and silently trained her soft, gray-blue eyes on mine with wordless understanding, as if she could see straight into my heart. What did I think? I could not explain my own compliant behavior, even to myself. I did not understand my own feelings.

The next time I saw Rupert, it was as if nothing had happened. Had I imagined it? Dreamed it? With no one to confide in and not knowing what it meant or how I felt about it, I consigned the incident to live forever in my book of days.

CHAPTER 3

THE TAILOR'S APPRENTICE

1810

As we had for ten years, Katy, Matilda, and I met in front of the baker's shop on the corner. This spring was just as glorious as ever, yet this spring was different. This was the last year we would be meeting each morning for carefree walks to school.

"I can't believe it's our last day of school!" Katy gushed with excitement.

"No more studies, no more books, no more teacher's dirty looks," Matilda sang.

I was less enthusiastic. I looked at my shoes and tried to catch some of my friends' excitement, but it wasn't working. I loved school and would have stayed in school forever if I could have. But I knew that no world existed in which I would be allowed to live that dream. I was neither wealthy nor male. I was fourteen, and my days as a schoolgirl were over. We were considered well educated. Most girls our age—the country girls, girls from poorer families, did not have the luxury of anything more than a rudimentary education.

Now that we had finished our studies, our families would certainly put us to some useful purpose. The only way I could be useful now was as my mother's domestic help. After all, most girls had been working at their mothers' sides since they were old enough to feed the backyard chickens, weed the garden, or scrub dirty clothes against the washboard. I did not look forward to a life of domestic drudgery. Mama tried to teach me the skills I needed, but she was an inconsistent teacher, sometimes laughing and enthusiastic, sometimes withdrawn and taciturn. I was an uninterested student, without domestic talent. I could boil potatoes, but Mama's delicious German potato salad was impossible for me to master. I could pull weeds, but I sometimes had difficulty telling the carrot tops from the parsley.

Mama's mood swings had affected our family in many ways. They even affected her appearance. Mama had a somewhat long face; a square jaw; soft, gray eyes; and thick, soft brown hair. She had been considered handsome, with a stately, composed demeanor. When I was a young child, I remember admiring her finely drawn, thin lips, slightly upturned at the corners, looking as if she was smiling internally at some private joke. But now, the corners of her lips sagged downward, and her smile looked forced. Outwardly, she was still calm and self-possessed, but her reticence masked a fragile spirit.

I could not imagine endless seasons under Mama's tutelage. When I pictured myself moving from kitchen to laundry to market, I felt like a horse in harness pulling a wagon of huge logs uphill through deep snow, or a yoked oxen plodding endlessly through rocky fields. Mama had returned to her normal household duties. She chatted with the other hausfrauen in the market, stoked the stove, cleaned, and cooked. But she only came fully alive when playing with Francisca. Francisca was her lifeline, in the same way I had been Gilly's. In my eyes, seven-year-old Francisca was long-limbed, plain, and unexceptional in every way. But Francisca and Mama were as close-knit as the stitches in one of Mama's tatted coverlets.

I found my escape in books. Books were rare in some families, but we were lucky. Father had a special arrangement with Herr Frankel, the itinerant bookseller who trawled up and down the Rhine River, from Baden-Baden to Basel, setting his nets for good, used books like fishermen trawled for silver carp. Father bartered salvage fabrics, imported thread, and his tailoring services for damaged or unsold books.

The bookseller was a man of the world, with refined literary tastes. He traveled widely and brought back the best he could find, both contemporary and classical volumes. Herr Frankel was a tall man, with long, disheveled, black hair streaked with gray and a long, wiry beard. His tall, flat-topped, black hat never left his head, and I'm quite sure I never saw the clothing he wore under the floor-length black overcoat he wore in all seasons. Hidden beneath his stern exterior was the soul of a wise, kindhearted sojourner.

Books were the only indulgence Father allowed himself. Sometimes

Father sacrificed a good night's sleep in favor of burying his nose in his latest acquisition, as he did with *The Sorrows of Young Werther* by Johann Wolfgang von Goethe, our most famous German writer. It was no longer a new book, but it was very popular the world over and the most widely read book in Germany. The leather cover of Father's book was weather-beaten, its pages well-worn and dog-eared. But the magic of the beautiful language and sad story were the same as when it was a new, gold-edged copy.

After Father set the book aside, I picked it up and brought it to the room I now shared with Francisca. I immersed myself in the soulful sufferings of young Werther and his tragic infatuation with a woman he could not marry. His life-ending despair only made me feel sorrier for my plight as a dreary hausfrau. Johann Wolfgang von Goethe captured my self-absorbed anxiety and made my imagined sufferings seem heroic.

One evening, when summer's oppression had defeated spring's optimism, I sat vacantly staring down at the street from our parlor window, gloomily pondering the hopelessness of my future. I saw Father hunched over, brows furrowed, shuffling through the street. Normally he returned from his guild meetings in a lighthearted mood, having passed a few hours enjoying a beer, conversation, and camaraderie with his peers. Though the air smelled of loam and peonies, the fullness of the season seemed to add to an invisible burden on Father's bowed shoulders. Father arrived home in a gloomy, pensive mood, so unlike him.

"Father, what can I get for you? *kaffekuchen*? A nice stein of lager?" Something was troubling him, and I hoped I could make him feel better.

"No, no liebchen. You cannot help with this problem. You see, a young journeyman schneider has applied to the guild to work in our town. They want me to bring him into my shop until he can complete his master work and qualify as a master schneider and set up his shop here. They don't think I can keep up with the tailoring needs of our growing town.

By now, Gruntal was large and prosperous enough to keep two schneidern busy. For hundreds of years, the guild had authorized only one tailor. But recently, Napoleon's soldiers had set up a camp on the outskirts of town, and they needed extra services. Our farms and businesses were thriving, and the population was increasing. A journeyman tailor from Freiburg was returning from his journey years. He had completed his apprenticeship several years earlier and then spent his three prescribed wander years, traveling the country taking temporary positions with master craftsmen, perfecting his skills, and gaining experience. Now he was ready to take one last journeyman position, produce his master work, and apply to the guild as master craftsman. The guild intended for him to settle here and open another shop.

The increased competition would surely reduce the number of our customers. People were happy with Father's work, but who knew how this new competitor would threaten us? A newcomer would surely attract attention and draw customers away from Father's business. How could Father impress upon the guild masters that he could handle the increased workload and that we did not need a new tailor? Father had never taken an apprentice and was reluctant to do so now. We had no extra room to take a journeyman under our roof, and even if we did, the extra work would strain Mama's nerves.

I could feel hope rising up in me, like the hopeful sap of trees in spring.

"But, Father, you have me! You know I am a good worker—good at sums and a fast learner. I have been doing small jobs for you for years. I know your customers, and they know me. I could do it. I could help you. I could be your apprentice. Other women have jobs. Frau Kopf is a midwife," I began, sounding more ardent than I intended.

"Well, of course! No man could be a midwife," Father countered. And he was right. That was not a good example.

"But I am strong and smart. You told me so. Boys begin their apprenticeships at my age or even younger. At school, I heard that a girl in Offenburg became an apprentice to the baker. I'm sure you know that the bookseller's wife manages his entire business when he travels on his book-buying journeys. There is no reason I could not do well as your apprentice."

"No, *schatzele*, you are a girl; your place is in the home."

Father's response was halfhearted. I didn't think he actually believed the words he spoke. I was undeterred by his arguments. The prospect of being a hausfrau filled me with dread. Not only would I be in constant contact with my inconstant mama but also my mind would wither. I would be old before I was seventeen.

After a long pause he said, "Well, I'll think about it."

He looked up at me standing over his shoulder. I was grinning encouragingly. His blue eyes regained their twinkle. A small smile coaxed the corners of his mouth upward. Though he said nothing, I knew the decision had already been made. Once again, I blessed my father's "modern" ideas.

At the next guild meeting, Father was prepared with his reasonable arguments. He strode off to the guild hall as the waning, late-summer light angled across the cobblestones and turned the half-timbered facades pale yellow.

I should not have heard Father's words. I should have been kneading bread. But my future seemed to hang in the balance. I was simultaneously fearful and excited. My heart beat in my throat, and my stomach tightened as I crouched beneath the open window. After nearly falling asleep while the burghers greeted each other and plodded through the stultifying preliminaries of the meeting, I heard my father's voice rise above the scraping of chairs and shuffling papers.

"Haven't I faithfully paid my dues and fees—on time and in full? Didn't I serve as pallbearer when Meister Kloster died last month, as I have done for many others before him? Hasn't my wife delivered meals to your family, Meister Klinke, when your wife was ill? I contributed generously to purchase the beautiful stained glass window our guild commissioned for the cathedral in Freiburg. Haven't I contributed in every way a good burgher might?"

Father was well loved and respected in the community. He was known for his charitable character. He epitomized the virtues of the guild's patron saint, Sankt Gutmann (the good man). He was scrupulously honest, generous to those in need, and a peacemaker in contentious circumstances. If his deposits into the bank of goodwill had been money, he would be the richest man in town.

"All I ask is that you give me a chance to prove Anastasia and I can fill our community's needs. You can always find a new tailor if our work is not adequate." With that, Father rested his case.

Many voices were raised against the idea. But the meisters knew there were precedents for a girl becoming an apprentice. It was rare but not unheard of. When the vote was taken, it was official. I would be the tailor's apprentice, the first female apprentice in our town. I was determined to be the best apprentice our town had ever known. My dream of a better future was revived. The journeyman would need to apply to the guild in another town.

September arrived with its swirling leaves and fecund harvest smells. I bustled down from our upstairs living quarters to the first-floor shop. The special aroma of linen, flax, and wool permeated the darkened space. The familiar, low-ceilinged room, with its ancient, rough-hewn table and woodstove for heating flatirons, felt new and exciting to me. I threw open the shutters to invite the bright autumn sun inside. The buttery glow of the slanting light penetrated even the most shadowy recesses of our shop. I busied myself making our shop cleaner and better organized than ever. I looked forward to each new day with joy and enthusiasm.

One day in early October, I was a bit late for our usually prompt early morning opening. The streets were alive with the town's commerce. The milk wagon rattled back to the dairy, having made its early morning deliveries. Buyers and sellers of every description hurried past, single-mindedly focusing on their appointed tasks. The baker, who started his day during the wee hours, filled the street with mouthwatering fragrances of fresh bread and *apfelkuchen*. I recalled meeting my friends every morning on that fragrant corner. My heart ached a bit as a brief wave of nostalgia passed through me. I realized my friends would not be there to meet me, not today, not ever.

"Guten Morgen, Frau Schmidt!" I hailed the old matron passing by as I opened the shutters. My heart was full of good cheer.

"Hello, Anastasia." My warm cheeriness bounced off her stony breast and back to me as cool suspicion.

I knew the people of the town were shocked. I felt their eyes upon me as I walked through the streets. I heard their whispers as I passed by. A new look in their eyes appraised my familiar features in a whole new light. The burden of their judgment hovered over my head like a living thundercloud, deciding if it should rain torrents of disapproval upon me or calmly blow over. I, Anastasia, was officially the tailor's apprentice. I understood getting used to this idea would be difficult for some of my friends and neighbors, but I would show them. I would be the best tailor's apprentice in the Schwarzwald.

Though I mourned for my lost school days, Father assured me that my education would continue in a different form. There would be records of guild meetings to keep, ledgers to balance, and correspondence from our suppliers and clients to read and respond to. All of this, he said, would make me an educated woman.

Father honored me by treating me as he would any boy. This meant he was sometimes testy and abrupt. He expected me to learn quickly, retain what I was told, and acquire all the skills I would need. Our success was important to our family, and I intended to earn his respect. When the shop's bell rang as a customer entered, I was the first person he or she saw. I greeted each customer with unfailing cheer. Each person's need—a ripped seam, an expanded waistband to accommodate a prosperous belly—was addressed respectfully. Every customer provided a lesson for me and for the good citizens of our town. A girl was perfectly capable of being a fine apprentice.

"Where is the *schneidermeister*?" blustered Herr Schwartz.

He was tall and round. He looked overfilled, like a pillow stuffed with too much goose down. I believed that what puffed him up so much was his own high opinion of himself. Undaunted by his cool greeting and even cooler attitude, I explained in my most cheerful tone. "Guten Tag, Herr Schwartz. I am the new apprentice. Please, tell me how I can help you."

"I need to see Herr Burkart. Get him! That's how you can help me." His voice was harsh, like boots on a gravel path.

Father emerged from the back of the workroom with a smile. His apron bristled with pins, giving him the appearance of a startled porcupine, quills at the ready. On this occasion, as in all others, Father included me in the conversation.

"Guten Morgen, Herr Schwartz. I see you have met my new apprentice." Father's smile did not waiver. "How may we help you?"

Herr Schwartz kept his eyes firmly fixed on Father, refusing to acknowledge me.

"This coat is so old it has become threadbare," he complained. "I need a new one, and I need it in two weeks."

"Apprentice, I need that new bolt of gray wool." Father ordered me about as if I was his soldier.

Like a dutiful aide-de-camp, I hustled to retrieve the requested bolt, emerging with a rich, gray worsted wool, the color of thunderclouds.

"Tell me, Herr Schwartz, is this the weight of fabric you want?" Father inquired.

"Yes, the weight seems right. But something else is wrong. I can't put my finger on it." I could see Herr Schwartz would not be easily pleased.

"Excuse me, sir. Is that the hat you normally wear at this time of year?" I asked quietly but not timidly.

"Yes, it is. Why do you ask?" Herr Schwartz looked straight ahead into the depths of the shop and pointedly away from me.

"May I show you another fabric?" My heart skipped in my chest. I was not frightened so much as excited by my own boldness.

"Go ahead, show us what you had in mind." Father was curious; a hint of amusement twinkled in his eyes.

I brought out another bolt of gray wool, but this one was a lighter shade, with flecks of black and tan. The overall effect was warm but livelier, less staid.

Herr Schwartz looked at the fabric and then at Father. "What do you think Meister Burkart?" he asked, still refusing to address me directly.

"My apprentice has a good eye for color and style," Father replied.

The good burgher finally looked me straight in the face and studied me carefully. I confined my gaze to the bolt of fabric. Herr Schwartz paused a long while.

"Yes, I would have to agree. This color is better suited to the color of my hat. I never would have thought of that." Now his tone was puzzled and a bit less blustery.

I raised my eyes to Herr Schwartz's. I was respectful but not obsequious. Herr Schwartz gave me a slight nod, tipped his hat, and left the shop. Little by little, one customer at a time, I was winning the respect of our townspeople.

In the evenings, I kept the books. Father greatly appreciated being relieved of this tiresome task. It gave him more time to read. After a few months of checking my work, he relaxed, knowing that errors were few and far between. Our novel situation became more comfortable for him and more rewarding for me. I walked the streets with a new stature that had nothing to do with the few inches I had grown.

After a time, the shock of seeing a female apprentice subsided. People saw me plying my new trade at the shop and at the fabric merchant's stall. Even the guild meisters congratulated themselves on their enlightened approval of the female apprentice.

At work, Father was still my tutor and taskmaster. We maintained a respectful, professional distance between us. He was "Meister Burkart" to me, and I was "Apprentice" to him. An overly chummy relationship would be viewed as inappropriate for a work situation and would cause our customers an itchy unease.

At home upstairs, we settled back into a comfortable familiarity. It was neither better nor worse than before. Or, I should say, it was both better and worse than it was when I was just a child. I missed his unguarded affection and being enveloped in his manly arms. These displays of affection were becoming rare. But that would have happened in any case as I turned into a young lady. As our relationship changed, a new, deeper bond emerged to take its place. I was more than just his oldest child, his daughter, his schatzele. I was his helper, his coworker, and his business partner. I was the tailor's apprentice.

Winter evenings were long and dark as they had always been. As the fire popped and cracked, Mama sat in its warmth, darning socks and rocking, with Francisca nestled in her lap. At five years old, Francisca was certainly too old for this babying. Father had the luxury of reading his most recent book, and I sat at the dining table, huddled over the ledgers.

Mama maintained her responsibilities as the household manager but with little enthusiasm. To all outward appearances, Mama behaved normally. Everything seemed routine during her good spells, but sometimes her old demons reemerged, engulfing her in stony silences. During those dark times, Mama sometimes lost the power of speech altogether. She walked through her days alive but not living. She neglected the house cleaning and avoided the other ladies in the market. Then she would suddenly reappear from her darkness and spin into a frenzy of cleaning, sewing new curtains for the house, or planting the neighborhood's most ambitious kitchen garden. Father always absolved her, but I was less forgiving.

"Mama has forgotten us. She doesn't love us anymore. The only one she cares about is Francisca," I whined.

"No, schatzele, you don't understand."

It warmed my heart to hear the familiar endearment he used less and less often. Hearing it again caused a strange lump to form in my throat.

"When you were only three years old, too young to remember, Mama and I lost another baby, our little Juliana. She was also born in winter like

Genoveva. Winter is a difficult time for babies and mothers. But the season was not to blame, as it was for our precious Genoveva. Juliana was born with a weak heart. She had dark hair, like you, and long, silky eyelashes. She was thin but beautiful, perfect in every way. She lived for only twenty-eight days; each day she grew more listless, and her heartbeat grew weaker. There was nothing anyone could do. You cannot understand the power of a mother's love or the overwhelming weight of the despair that stabs the heart like an assassin's rapier. I hope you will never experience this trial."

Deep in the recesses of my mind, I tried to conjure up an image of a beautiful, dark-haired baby with long lashes. Perhaps I didn't remember Juliana because Mama had not withdrawn from me when she died, as she had when Genoveva died. Or maybe I was too young to carry that pain in my soul. Many women lost babies. Many women hid their mourning inside their hearts, sheltering it from prying eyes, like a hawk shelters its prey beneath its wings, while they presented a stoic face to the world. Mama remained present for me when Juliana died, so I soon forgot the dead baby. But Mama did not forget. Two years after Juliana died, our Gilly, was born, our happy, handsome little boy. Mama's dead babies lived in her heart like empty rooms that can never be filled again.

Francisca seemed to sense Mama's great need for comfort and clung to Mama during her dark periods. For Mama, Francisca's life was accompanied by the ghosts of dead babies. Mama's dark fear of another lost baby made her fiercely attentive to Francisca.

I detached myself from my need for a mother's support. I had Father's support, and that was enough. I was confident that I was strong-willed and resilient enough to support myself. I had responsibilities and skills Mama had never experienced. As I had hoped, I inhabited a world totally different than hers.

At the shop, I graduated to taking measurements, and basting the seams for alterations. Finally, Father allowed me to put my sharpest scissors ever so carefully to fine cloth. Knowing how much fabrics cost, it terrified me to make that first, irrevocable cut into the fine linen and wool Father so painstakingly sought out. But it was also thrilling. Like a well-tailored garment, the life of a craftsman was a perfect fit for me.

CHAPTER 4

SAYING GOODBYE

1811

My little Gilly was growing up. He was no longer little Gilly but simply brother Gilly. Most evenings, when lamps were lit and mothers called for their children, he was carousing with his many school friends. He was renowned for his sense of humor and practical jokes.

One spring day, when he was nine years old, he glued a trail of pfennigs to the walk leading to the school. He hid in the bushes as his friends struggled to pick them up. They got grumpier and grumpier until Gilly gave his position away, unable to contain his giggles. His friends descended upon him, giving him a hearty but harmless thumping. He was loved by all his friends, though less loved by his meisters. Even so, there were some whose frigid exterior melted a little when his humor and quick wit caught them by surprise. His playfulness overshadowed his academic prowess. He was certainly capable of better marks in school but not concerned when he fell short of Father's expectations.

Over time, as Mama continued to shower most of her attention on Francisca, sparing only wayward drops for Gilly and myself, Gilly's behavior became progressively more riotous. It began with little things, like stealing cookies from the cookie jar when he was four, pulling the unripe turnips from Frau Dorner's garden when he was seven, and shooting pebbles at the girls with his peashooter when he was eight. When he was ten, Gilly incited Rupert Schultz's little brother, Clem, to take one of the Belgians out of the barn without permission, tie ropes around its neck, and whip it up to speed as they bounced behind on the toboggan.

Eventually his high jinks had turned truly risky. Last summer, at the height of breeding season, he climbed the fence into the pasture where Herr Schultz confined his huge bull. The great beast, who was naturally ill-tempered, became a raging giant during breeding season. Everyone knew that no one could go near him, except perhaps a cow. Gilly poked at the bull with a long stick and then ran in circles to see if he could make the huge creature dizzy. It didn't take long before the two thousand-pound beast was upon him. It was something of a miracle that Herr Schultz noticed what was going on, and courageously placed himself between Gilly's prostrate body and the bull's sharp horns. Gilly fled back over the fence, but Herr Schultz suffered a serious laceration in his leg. Gilly's prank was no longer funny. Infection from such a wound could easily kill a man. Herr Schultz confronted Father, exhorting him to control his son's hazardous behavior.

Now, Gilly's pranks had become difficult for Mama and Father to control. In 1811, Gilly was eleven, and they decided that it would be a good experience for him to spend the summer at the farm of Mama's sister, Maria Francisca, and her husband, Franz Dorner. Their names had been a kind of a family joke; everyone referred to them as Franz and Franz. Mama's sister was one of our favorite relatives. She was short and stout, with frizzy hair she could never control and a hearty laugh. But she could be stern too. I'm sure this was necessary to keep order in her family of ten children; a large, prosperous farm; and a husband who did not tolerate disobedience.

It seemed like the perfect match for Gilly. He would have plenty of physical work, cousins to romp with, and an aunt and uncle who were both friendly and strict. Mama and Father hoped Gilly would gain a sense of responsibility and some maturity by spending the summer at the farm. Gilly's escapades scared me, too. But he was old enough now that he no longer paid much attention to his big sister. So as soon as school classes had ended, Gilly was packed off to the countryside.

It was a hot, June afternoon. The water pitcher sweated out its last bit of coolness in the still, sultry air. Though it was barely past spring, it felt like the height of summer. Gilly had been gone for only a few weeks when Uncle Franz galloped up to our door, spurring his dray horse to speeds it had not achieved since it was a colt. Father emerged from his workshop, bristling with the usual assortment of pins, the measuring tape draped around his neck. I followed him upstairs, leaving the door open and the shop unattended.

"Why, Franz, what an unexpected pleasure. Come in and have some kaffeekuchen," Father greeted Franz warmly.

"Franz, how nice to see you." Mama was delighted but puzzled when Franz vaulted up the stairs and burst into the kitchen. Why would her hard-working brother-in-law leave his fields in the middle of the growing season?

Without any polite preliminaries, he commanded Mama. "You must come and get Gilly."

"What's wrong? What has that boy done now?" Mama's voice dropped into a lower register, panic growing in her eyes. My own heart rattled madly against my ribs.

"No, he has been a pleasant addition to our household. That's not it. Some of the children have become ill. Their throats are swollen. They have headaches."

A dark, ominous look passed from Uncle Franz's face to Mama's and then to Father's. They seemed to share a secret knowledge of these symptoms. And that knowledge apparently filled them with horror and a terrible sense of urgency.

"I will go back to the farm with you and bring him home immediately," Father said, without a moment's hesitation, without a thought of the tailor shop or making preparations.

Father left to saddle up our aging horse. Mama sat Uncle Franz down in the kitchen, settled a plate of kuchen before him, and set about making sandwiches with fat slabs of *butterkase* cheese and thick slices of ham on substantial rounds of pumpernickel to sustain the men on their hurried trip back to the farm.

"This could not have come at a worse time." Franz toyed with the delicious plum kuchen with his fork but did not eat a bite.

"The calves need to be weaned soon. The hay in the fields needs constant attention. Gilly, lively as he is, made a good worker when paired up with my Wilhelm. The two of them made it all a game but got the work finished. I don't know how I will manage without my sons' help."

Worry crept back into his voice, which trailed off as his eyes stared sightlessly at his boots. He dropped his head into his hands, and his shoulders shook, though no sound escaped from his grim lips.

"Are they *all* sick?" Alarm lit up Mama's face. She envisioned her dear sister Francisca's ten children.

"So far, it's only the older boys. They all share the big room in the attic." He paused. His shoulders slumped. His calloused hands lay limp in his lap as he shook his head. "I just can't make it without them."

Franz had a small but prosperous dairy farm and cheese house. He grew hay for the cows and vegetables to sustain his large brood. Although it was nothing like the multifaceted Schultz operation, it was fruitful enough for his hardworking family. He relied on his children to supply labor, as many small farmers did.

Mama, Francisca, and I watched from the front door as Father and Franz spurred their lumbering horses, bred for heavy work, not speed. The next day, Father returned with Gilly propped in front of him on the old horse. Gilly's face was flushed and his eyes glassy. He looked like he had a cold, though it was not the season for colds. He was impassive as Father threw him over his shoulder like a sack of potatoes and brought him upstairs.

Mama immediately descended on Gilly like one of the furies of legend, swept him up into her arms, and deposited him in bed. I would never have imagined Mama having the strength to lift Gilly, who was no longer a small boy, but she carried him as if he was weightless. Her fear gave her a strength only terror can impart.

"Mama, what is it? What's the matter with Gilly?" I hugged Francisca to my side possessively.

"It's the pox!" Mama's voice was thick and low, hardly recognizable. The very word conjured up horrid images. Every year thousands of people died of the dreaded pox, most of them children.

Mama tried every remedy she had ever heard about to alleviate his suffering, hoping that he would be one of the lucky few who survived the ferocious disease. She applied cold compresses to his head for his fever, plied him with a concoction of barley and sorrel roots with a little saffron added, and anointed his eyes with rose water to which a few drops of pigeon blood had been added. Mama hung a sheet around Gilly's bed. She gathered up the few toys that he kept as cherished relics of his young boyhood and pitched them into the fire. She did the same with his bedding. Francisca and I were forbidden to get close to him. Poor Gilly suffered in isolation, one old blanket wrapped around him, with only his pillow for comfort.

After about a week, livid pustules covered his head and torso. An alarming rash on his tongue prevented him from eating or drinking. Mama's eyes gleamed with terror. Soon Gilly could no longer rise from his bed. He became feverish; his muscles ached. The only sounds we heard coming from his cocoon were his low moans.

One evening I snuck into his curtained refuge. I wanted to comfort my little brother, my childhood shadow, my friend, but Mama swept in to separate us.

"Get back! Stay away! I've seen this disease before!" Mama roughly pulled her blouse off her shoulder. The skin on her neck and shoulder was speckled with whitish pits. Then I understood. Smallpox had already touched her life.

The mere mention of smallpox sent as much fear through a community as an invading foreign army. The word itself was used as a curse. "A pox on you!" was one of the most wounding blows an enemy could hurl. The voracious disease consumed people of all ages, but its greatest appetite was for children.

Mama would not allow anyone, not even Father, into Gilly's enclosure. She knew she could not be sickened because, as a child, she had survived the curse. As a recovered sufferer, she enjoyed some protection from the disease. Like the milkmaids who sometimes contracted cowpox, a mild form of the disease, she knew she would be immune.

Little Francisca, with the understanding of a six-year-old, could not comprehend the danger of the disease. In tears, she confessed to me that one night she'd crept past his curtained enclosure and held his hand. She'd laid her cheek against his barely moving chest. The horror of seeing his body covered with blistering spots was more than she could bear. She sobbed in my arms because she was afraid to confess her indiscretion to Mama. For a week, Francisca had night terrors. Her screams were like one possessed, and she could not be silenced. She wedged her small body into a corner, her eyes wide but unseeing. She was neither awake nor asleep but trapped in some netherworld of hellish visions. Nothing could shake her out of her purgatory.

Then, merely two weeks after coming home from the farm, Gilly was gone. Our perfect, funny, charming, wild Gilly—gone. The family mourned within the prison of grief that the walls of our home had become. Our friends and neighbors brought plates of food and left them at our doorstep, afraid to venture inside our cursed dwelling. Father Dinny even refused to come inside to administer the last rites for poor Gilly. We could not give our sweet, silly boy a decent funeral because we knew people would flee from us if we walked the streets, afraid that even his dead body would spread contagion. Father's guild friends offered condolences by pinning notes to our door, now draped with black crepe. The neighborhood hausfrauen left potato dumplings and spaetzle to comfort us. Matilda Kohler and Katy Herr placed a bouquet of wildflowers and a note especially for me on our doorstep.

Mama would not allow us to see or touch his body. She wrapped Gilly in the old blanket that had comforted him in his last days, draped his shell of a body over the saddle horn of the old horse, and plodded off alone, leading the old horse by his tether. She buried him in the pauper's cemetery, three miles from our town. Only the grave diggers were present to witness his burial. The only record of his passing was the terse entry in the Rastatt township records that bookended his short life – Igidius Burkart, 3 September 1800 to 23 July 1811. Our Gilly was gone.

We continued to quarantine ourselves for the two weeks following Gilly's death as the local custom required. We grieved. We ate little. Father puttered in the shop, cleaning and organizing his stock. But mainly, he sat uselessly in the upholstered chair, head in hands. Tears interrupted any attempts we made at conversation. We waited. The specter of death hung about the house. We could feel it looking us over like a starving man in a bakeshop, considering which tasty morsel he would devour next.

Within another week, the now-familiar progression of suffering began again, this time with Francisca. From the deepest well of grief, panic rose. The spikes of insufferable sorrow stabbed our hearts like Jesus's crown of thorns.

It was late summer when Francisca took ill. Though the house was sweltering, windows and doors remained locked tight. Mama would not leave Francisca's side. Father and I begged Mama to eat and rest, but she would not, could not. She had already lost three of her five children. If strength of will alone could beat back the enemy, Mama would stare down the devil himself.

The next two weeks passed in unrelenting gloom. We could do nothing but pray.

* * *

Miraculously, Francisca did not die. Mother's fierce tenacity defied the evil forces trying to take her from us as they had taken Gilly. Mama had faced the angel of death again and, this time, sent it slinking back to hell. After two weeks, Francisca emerged, still alive but changed. Small, white depressions scarred her beautiful, pale child's skin. They trailed up her arms, ran across her neck, and blemished her sweet face. When Francisca was a baby, she'd saved Mama's life by giving her a reason to keep living. Now Mama had saved Francisca. But the specter of death left scars that would change us forever—scars on poor Francisca that would change the course of her life, scars on Mama and Father that they would carry on their souls, and scars on my heart, deep grooves where sorrow would settle when it revisited my life.

But as scarred as we were, we needed to carry on. Our business had suffered because our customers were afraid to knock on the shop door, knowing that the family living above was poxed and dangerous.

Finally, the torrid, hellish summer loosen its grip. September finally arrived and brought a breath of cooler, fresh air. We struggled to return to our normal life. Mama opened the windows. I sewed clean new bedding for all of us. Once again, I threw open the shop's shutters in the morning, greeting everyone in the street. Father resumed his guild responsibilities, assuring the town leaders that the danger had passed.

"As bad as it was," I heard him explain to Herr Schwartz, "we never endangered any other family. We voluntarily suffered a self-imposed quarantine." He left unsaid the plea that we not be ostracized.

"Yes, I suppose you're right," Herr Schwartz replied. "No one else has gotten sick. So at least you did not spread your misfortune."

And this was true. The hangman's knot loosened. Our routine gradually returned to its familiar rhythm.

I made it a point to talk to everyone I encountered, doing my best to appear cheerful and healthy. I visited the fabric merchants and confidently placed new orders. I did the same with the notions seller, ordering thread and carefully choosing an assortment of buttons that would tempt our customers. Eventually our patrons returned. Their alternative would have been to make the inconvenient, time-consuming journey to Baden-Baden, several miles away. By the time the holiday season arrived, our business had returned to normal.

Francisca had changed in ways deeper than scarred skin. She became withdrawn and refused to go back to school. She resumed clinging to Mama, curling up in her lap at every opportunity like a spoiled housecat. Mama never rejected any of Francisca's clinging behavior. Though Mama never returned to her bed, face turned to the wall as she had when Genoveva died, her eyes were hollow. Her movements were mechanical like the windup toys I saw at the Christmas market.

Papa's suffering was like a puncture wound. On the surface, it looked like a small hole poked in the skin. But beneath the surface, his distress festered and burned, made worse by that peculiar male pride that prevented him from outwardly showing his pain. He acted out his suffering, displaying an uncharacteristically bad temper—a curse mumbled beneath his breath when he dropped his scissors, a slammed door, behaviors I had never seen in him before Gilly's death.

That winter, the fire burned in the hearth as it always had. I worked at the ledger books, taking special care to involve Francisca in my work so she could learn her sums. Father retreated more into his books, and Mother silently darned socks and swept floors. Our quarters were quiet; the muted scrape of my quill over paper, the muffled shush of pages being turned, the swish of the broom, or the creak of Mama's rocking chair only accentuated the silence.

On one of those silent, empty nights, I had a visitation from Gilly. I suppose it might be called a dream, as I had been sleeping. But I felt as if I was fully awake. Gilly stood at the foot of my bed, grinning. He was as real and fully present to me as he ever had been. He was singing one of his favorite songs, a funny poem about an unlucky hunter who ended up being chased by the deer he hunted. He laughed and made faces. He filled me with joy and peace. Then he was gone. I realized I was sitting up in bed, eyes wide open with a huge smile on my face and happy tears in my eyes.

"Thank you, Gilly. You came to tell me you are fine. You came to say goodbye," I whispered. "Goodbye, my sweet brother. You will always be with me."

CHAPTER 5

THE CONSCRIPTION

1812

My work consumed most of my daylight hours and some evenings as well. But there were many opportunities for socializing. I outgrew the children's choir at St. Michaels, but I continued to sing with the adult choir. The high, light soprano voice of my childhood had mellowed into a slightly lower range. Rupert Schultz's voice had inevitably changed too. The vocal purity only a boy chorister could possess was replaced by a rich, resonant baritone. He was invited to join the Liederkranz Society, as I might have been if they allowed women. While I still sang the sacred high Mass in St. Michael's, Rupert was preparing for the *sangerfest*, where dozens of men's singing groups from all around the area would come together and compete for top honors.

Rupert and I had grown closer. That first brush of lips grew into a deeper attraction. Sometimes we sang together, holding hands and trying to achieve beautiful harmony. Most often, we broke into uncontrollable laughter. Soon he asked my father's permission to visit me, take me for walks, and accompany me to our town festivals. Father and Mama in turn invited him for Sunday dinner. And why not? Our families had a long friendship. Rupert had good prospects for the future; Herr Schultz ran a prosperous farm. In addition to growing a wide variety of vegetables and keeping a small dairy herd, he was renowned for the prized grapes he used to produce his signature Riesling wines. As the oldest in his family, Rupert, the heir apparent of his family's farm, was already well versed in viticulture and the business of running the farm. We were too young to marry but maybe not too young to court. I was sixteen and Rupert eighteen.

Rupert was not beautiful. He was ordinary by most physical measures, average height and build, passably good looking, but not an Adonis. To my eyes, though, he was perfect. His wavy blond hair had not darkened. His bluest blue eyes and crooked smile were still irresistible. I was considered comely but not lovely like my mother. Where she was above average height and elegant but fragile, I was small and slim but also strong and hardy. My dark hair contrasted nicely with my hazel eyes, or so I was told. Other girls were considered genuine beauties, like Katy Herr. Katy was born beautiful. Her entire life she had been greeted with unsought praise, as though being pretty was a personal accomplishment and not just an accident of fortune. Katy, to her credit, was largely unmoved by the flattery she received. If anything, the unwelcomed attention made her a little less outgoing, more wary, especially around boys.

Spring blanketed the forest floor with tiny spring beauties. Budding spring green leaves had not yet enclosed the canopy. As they did every year, the young farmers' sons started searching each family's woodlot to find the straightest, tallest, most impressive tree for our Maypole. It took many strong, young backs to fell the tree, bring it out of the woods, and skin the bark off until the pole was as smooth as a sausage. After it was prepared, they brought it to the village square on the eve of May Day.

From ages past, a time before remembering, people eagerly awaited the coming of spring and celebrated the return of life, light, and all new things. Our ancient ancestors believed the stately firs of the Schwarzwald had souls. They revered the trees as symbols of our connection to mother earth, decorating them in winter and spring and planting new trees to celebrate births, marriages, and deaths. What better symbol of the season than the stalwart Maypole!

The May Day festivities began early in the day. The young men competed to make the giant maypole as beautiful as it could be, adding colorful ribbons, wreaths, and symbols so old no one recalled their meaning. The finishing touch was attaching a string of our best bratwurst to the highest point. After the pole was transformed into an elegant monolith, the strongest of the young men took their places alongside the huge pole. Little by little, to the accompaniment of the band and the encouragement of the crowd, they used long poles to raise the sleeping giant to its full glory. When it finally stood tall with its base firmly grounded in the earth, a wild howl went up from the crowd. The band struck up its liveliest tunes, and the fun began.

The most agile of the boys took turns climbing the limbless, tree trying to reach the sausages at the top. One after the other, they slid back down, their enthusiasm exceeding their strength. Finally, Rupert, neither the strongest nor the most agile, took his turn. He carefully inched up the pole, planning each move, until he just barely caught hold of the lowest dangling sausage. It tumbled down on his head and hit the ground well before Rupert completed his descent. The other boys draped the sausages around his neck like a garland, laughing and slapping his back. They lifted him on their shoulders and paraded him around in circles, the bratwurst king of spring.

Now it was the girls' turn. Each of us chose a young man and placed one of the colorful ribbons in his hand. I dove into the crowd to snatch my Rupert's hand before any other girl had a chance. Together we took our places, boys and girls alternating, circling the tree while facing in opposite directions. As we wove our ribbons around the tree, the crowd cheered and sang. I laughed into my Rupert's eyes. He responded with his funny, crooked smile. I felt certain we were weaving our lives together as surely as we wove the ribbons around the pole. Kegs of the dark, sweet maibock were tapped, and we danced all day to polkas and waltzes.

As the sun slipped down to meet the dark hills, Rupert and I crept from the crowd. We found a quiet bench near the edge of town, where the river that created our pond in winter now swelled with the melting snow from the high hills above. The flowery scent that flavored the spring air also flavored our stolen kisses. This time, they were true, mutual kisses, not accidental but entirely, sincerely shared. We strolled back to the crowd hand in hand, in front of his family, my family, and the entire town. We could not have declared our love any louder if we had stood on the bandstand and shouted.

Our town continued to celebrate, dance, and sing. We were the lucky ones. We knew that many other cities and towns were embroiled in war and misery. The gazettes Herr Frankel brought from across the Rhine spoke of battle after battle. Britain, Spain, Portugal, Belgium, Poland, and even faraway Sweden were battle scarred. Napoleon's war machine was rolling over the continent. Napoleon's incessant wars were a constant source of fretful debate among the citizens. Women were not expected to educate themselves about foreign wars, but Father took me into his confidence, recounting the topics being discussed by the burghers and involving me in discussion.

Since our rulers had thrown in their lot with Napoleon in 1806, we had enjoyed a nervous peace. We hoped our fragile alliance would protect us. French military officers and government officials occasionally visited our town, conferring with local officials. These imperious Napoleonic overlords, who previously needed us to make their new shirts and sell them sausages, now took what they wanted and bullied the residents. They clearly wanted to demonstrate their power over us. What they wanted in 1812 was an army. What they took were our young men.

In early June, Rupert's brother, Clem, exploded into the shop, so breathless he could hardly form words. "They've taken him! They have him! He's going to war!" He did not wait for a reply but sped off to his family's home to alert them.

My blood froze in my veins. I dropped the trousers I was altering and flew to the camp on the edge of town where troops, conscripted from our town, marched up and down a makeshift parade ground, training for Napoleon's army. I flew at the soldier guarding the training grounds, pounding my fists against the white sashes crossed over his chest. The single-minded force of my assault nearly propelled me past the guardsman. Though I had surprised him at his post, he seized my two arms and held me tightly enough to raise bruises. I was oblivious to the pain. I barely saw the soldier who squeezed my arms in his viselike grip. I saw only the young men of our town, our neighbors and friends, lined up at the army induction table. There they were being conscripted into the "Grande Armee" to do Napoleon's dirty work.

"Rupert! Rupert! Run!" I screamed. "Run! Get away from them!"

Heads turned in my direction. I was a crazed girl screaming impossible commands to a sweetheart already caught in the snare of Napoleon's web.

But it was far too late. Even if it were possible, running would have done no good at all. If he ran away, the overwhelming might of Napoleon's minions would have forcibly retrieved him. Every village and town across our area had its own version of this scene. The markets, taverns, guild halls, and streets buzzed with fearful rumors of how, like a huge, clinging leech, Napoleon's never-ending wars across Europe were sucking the blood from our communities.

That evening as I lay across my bed, sobbing helplessly, Father tried to console me. "You know, schatzele, we've been lucky. In towns all over Europe—in Italy, Belgium, and Spain—there have been battles and war. We have tried to make peace with Napoleon, and he has rewarded us by leaving us more or less untouched by the savagery that's been going on for years in other places. Napoleon is a strong leader, practically invincible. Rupert and the others will be home by Christmas, showing off their medals for bravery."

"But no! They can't take him! Where are they going?" I wailed. "What will his father do without him on the farm? He belongs here!"

"They're marching to fight the Russians, who don't have a prayer against the might of Napoleon's army." Father tried to sound optimistic.

But there was no consoling me. I pulled Father's heavy atlas down from the bookshelf. Russia was 2,500 kilometers away! How could anyone, even Napoleon's army, walk that far!

Father was right. Napoleon had ravaged many countries across the continent. He engaged in so many wars that his own country could no longer supply all the soldiers his voracious empire-building consumed. We, as a vassal state, now paid dearly for our "peace." His swaggering officers marched their strutting horses down the main street to meet with the civil authorities. The following week, the conscription tables appeared outside towns across the area. Within a few months, there were so few young men left that we worried who would bring in the harvest. In our little corner of Germany alone, almost seven thousand soldiers marched off to war, nearly every eligible young man.

On a drizzly June day, we saw them off. It had been a cool, wet spring. The boys' new wool uniforms and tall, black boots were spattered with mud before they had marched even one kilometer down the road leading toward Russia. Mothers wrung their hands in anxiety. Little brothers danced alongside the cortege, cheering and waving their hats in the air. Young wives with babes in arms whose young husbands were stripped from their embrace wailed inconsolably. I stood quietly on the green verge about a half kilometer outside of town where the crowd thinned out.

Rupert marched methodically, mechanically, his eyes looking straight ahead. His face was pale, his clothes, a little too small for his lean, muscular body. His body. The thought of it sent a surge of blood to my face and unleashed a stream of silent, relentless tears. As if there was a magnetic force drawing us together, his head turned toward me. My eyes locked on his. In this brief moment, time stood still. The clamor of drums and soldiers' boots seemed to fade. Rupert turned his impossibly blue eyes to mine. They were wide with fear. My hazel eyes blurred as they filled with tears. In that moment, our hearts belonged to each other completely. Our souls were one, as if they had been together in eternity and would always be so.

There was no consoling me. Unleashed devils of despair ravaged my soul. The face of evil stared ravenously into my world. The face was Napoleon's. The senseless viciousness of war led me down the dark path from which there is no return to innocence. I walked through my days as if asleep, alive but not living. I exuded an inky blackness that repelled everyone who came near me. I abandoned myself to my grief. Finally, I understood the black moods my mother suffered. I forgave her completely.

Despite my broken heart, my responsibilities did not allow me the luxury of shirking my work. For me, there would be no days and nights in bed, face turned toward the wall while my family suffered from neglect. Now, more than ever, the family needed me.

My heart ached for all the other wives, mothers and sisters I had seen weeping on the roadside. I sympathized with the stoic, silent fathers for whom the loss of their male heirs, their pride and joy, left gaping holes in their hearts and lives. I wanted to comfort them, to let them know they were not alone. One evening, as I was struggling to focus on the columns of numbers before me, I conceived a plan.

"Father, do you remember that bolt of block-printed, cotton muslin we have on the back shelf in the storeroom?" I tried to introduce my idea to Father gently, in a way he would be able to accept.

"Hmmm ..." Father mumbled.

"Father, did you hear me?" I persisted.

He looked up, a bit surprised. "Did you say something, schatzele?"

"Yes, I did. Do you think we will have a use for that remnant bolt of printed muslin that has been sitting at the back of the storeroom for two years?" I began.

"What about it?" He was wary but curious.

"My heart aches for Frau Schultz and the other women who watched their sons march off to war. Some of those families will be shorthanded at harvest. Craftsmen who have lost their apprentices will suffer. And I have an idea of how I can help comfort them."

"Yes, you have a good heart. I know you are suffering too. But what does that have to do with the bolt of block-printed muslin? It's no good. There was a flaw in the printing, and the pattern is not perfectly applied."

"Yes, exactly! Since we can't use it for another purpose, I would like to make simple aprons for the women of town. I think it would be a nice gesture."

Father's blue eyes augered into my very heart. I forthrightly returned his gaze and did not look away.

"I suppose it would do no harm. We can't use the fabric elsewhere. But when could you possibly find time?"

"I'll work on those evenings when I am not keeping the books. The sewing will be easy. I'll embroider some simple flowers along the waistband and add a pocket in front. I think it will be appreciated."

"Indeed, I believe it will. Your resourcefulness never ceases to amaze me." He smiled weakly.

One Sunday afternoon, after the pale greens of late spring changed into the deep greens of early summer, I knocked at the door of my schoolgirl friend, Matilda Kohler. Her father, Hermann Kohler, was the baker, a generous, pleasant man, who often joined the young people in winter's skating fun. Matilda's brother, Friedrich (we had called him Fritz) had marched off to war with my Rupert and all the others.

"Guten Tag, Frau Kohler," I greeted Matilda's mother as she opened the door to me.

At the sound of my voice, Matilda came running. "Anastasia! It's you!" She greeted me with a hug. She looked older.

We had been out of school for four years, and though we still occasionally saw each other at the market and festivals, the daily responsibilities we now shouldered isolated us from each other. Her hair was disheveled. Her round, rosy face seemed longer and paler. She rushed to embrace me. Flour from her apron smeared over my Sunday dress.

"Oh, look what I've done." She brushed the front of my dress with her floury hands, making my dark grey worsted skirt a powdery, white mess. She looked desperately up into my eyes, worried I would be angry. When our eyes met, the spark of schoolgirl silliness reignited, and we recognized the ridiculous comedy unfolding. I started to giggle as I joined her in brushing off my skirt. She giggled too, and for a moment, we were transformed back into the happy girls we once had been.

"What brings you here?" Her father smiled as he emerged from the kitchen.

"I have brought a gift for Frau Kohler and Matilda." I ceremoniously presented the folded package, wrapped in cheesecloth and tied with twine.

The meticulously embroidered aprons suddenly seemed like an empty gesture, oddly out of balance with the seriousness of the situation.

"It's not much," I apologized, "but I wanted to offer some small gesture to Frau Kohler. I know she must be, you all must be, desperate with worry now that Fritz is no longer in the safety of your home. I hoped this small gesture would be of comfort." I blathered too many words, more than were necessary. I could not tell if the sincerity of my gift was foolish or simply irrelevant. My cheeks heated up as I dropped my head and looked at my shoes, eyes burning with sorrow and embarrassment.

"Well," said the good baker, "you are just like your father, thinking of the well-being and happiness of others."

I blushed, proud to be compared to my father.

"Come in, come in." Frau Kohler took my hand and pulled me into their home. "You must have some of our kuchen. It's still warm, just out of the oven. It is so refreshing to see you again."

We spent an hour in the delicious warmth of their kitchen, as the little ones played at our feet. We spoke of the price of flour from the mill, how the younger children were doing in school, the unusually cool weather, everything except Napoleon's war and the absence of our sons, brothers, and sweethearts.

For the next month, I delivered the simple aprons to other women I knew were grieving along with me. The surprise in their eyes and the smiles on their lips were the best possible rewards I could have had.

June wore on. The lupines and edelweiss bloomed as usual. The pines and firs on the slopes exuded a heady aroma of rising sap. But the fertility of nature did not bring me joy as it always had. There was nothing hopeful in the exuberant growth as the season turned through its timeless cycle of renewal, heedless of our suffering.

Spring bled into summer. It was an unusually rainy, cool summer. Though the town market was strangely subdued that summer, marketing days took on a new importance. It was a chance for us to exchange as much information as we could. Very little of it was actual news; most of what we heard was only rumor. But we shared every scrap of information we could glean. We knew it was very difficult for our men and boys to send a letter home. Judging by what we had heard from the few post riders who customarily traveled from one inn to another delivering messages, the roads were in terrible condition, muddy and rutted. Thousands of troops with their horses and wagons churned them into ankle-deep quagmires. It was almost impossible to negotiate roads choked with troops and beset by brigands whose ruined lives turned them into outlaws.

By late August, the air was already cool. The summer had been chilly and wet. I bustled through the crowded aisles of the market, concentrating on my shopping list. This week, we needed both cotton and silk thread and three sizes of sewing needles.

I spotted my old friend. "Katy Herr!" I shouted and waved. "Katy, how are you? How is your family?" I rushed to catch her before she left the market.

Katy's father was a shoemaker. Katy was the youngest, with four older brothers. Two of them had marched off to the Russian front with Rupert. One of the two remaining brothers stayed at home. He was sweet and well loved, but feebleminded and of little use to the army or the shoemaker. The oldest brother had lost the bottom half of a leg after a sledding accident several years ago, when a broken bone had become gangrenous and had to be amputated. He was surly and irascible but could sit at the worktable and help his father.

I was shocked by Katy's appearance. She had just turned seventeen but looked thirty. Her sunken eyes were dull. Her beautiful, wavy tresses hung feebly over her ears. Her hands were chafed, her expression severe. Small lines sprouted between her eyes, testimony to the recent years of worry and work. She was wearing the apron I had sewn for her. Dark berry juice stains swam through greasy blotches of lard on its flowered fabric. She wore the wooden clogs of a washerwoman.

"How is your mother? Have you heard anything from your brothers?" I blurted.

Katy spoke slowly. "Do you remember when you swore you would not become a hausfrau? We all laughed at you then. What could be wrong with keeping house?" Her voice had a hard edge of disillusionment.

I had not expected this comment. "Actually, I knew you thought I was a little strange for liking school, but I didn't know you laughed at me." I wondered why she'd led the conversation down this path.

"Well we did," she said bluntly, not caring how her words might wound me. "But I'm not laughing now. My two strong brothers are gone. My father works day and night. Berthold, do you remember him? He's almost thirty and a cripple. He struggles, working with my father and trying to keep our business going."

"And you? What of you?" I was concerned. Her blunt tone and her appearance did not resemble the happy schoolgirl I remembered.

"I am now a hausfrau, toiling in the kitchen garden, in the washroom, and tending Hermann. Do you remember him? He's my idiot brother. What I wouldn't give to have a skill or craft that involved more than stooping and grunting!"

Her unpleasant words rattled me. Something was wrong. She had never been unkind, insensitive, or as unsparingly blunt as she was now.

She looked at me with empty eyes. "We've gotten a letter from Peter's superior officer. He's dead. And Bernhard is missing." The unvarnished power of her words hit my chest as though I had been punched.

"Oh, my dear, dear Katy …" I moved to embrace her.

"Don't!" she barked. "Have you spoken to Frau Schultz lately?"

I froze in my tracks.

I turned abruptly and ran without a word, my errands forgotten. I found Frau Schultz in the parlor staring into space, the rest of the children weeping at her knees. Herr Schultz stood stoop-shouldered at the window, hands clasped behind his back.

Wordlessly she showed me the letter:

July 1812

Dear Father, Mother, family, and dearest Anastasia,

If this letter reaches you, please know that God has taken pity on me, and my soul still inhabits my body. I am luckier than many. Peter Herr fell ill from stomach poisoning, probably from the bluish-black meat we ate for wont of any other provision. I haven't seen Bernhard since we crossed into Poland. No one has.

We left Gruntal fat, but hunger has gnawed away any extra flesh we had. We fast-marched for many weeks and are now across the Vistula River. We marched so fast and far we overtook our supply wagons. Now, we fend for ourselves for food, digging up potatoes and chasing dogs for meat. The farther east we go, the poorer the country becomes. Now we share the poverty of the poor farmers, who stare at us hollow-eyed or flee before us, leaving nothing behind for our provisioning. The Polish farms are stark, and their crops are meager. The people seem to me like backward peasants from ages past.

It has rained a cold, unrelenting rain for the past five days. The roads, already poor, are a morass of mud. Not one stitch of my clothing has been dry for weeks. At night, we pile ourselves together like puppies at the teat to keep from freezing. There is no shelter from the storms. The lice that inhabit our bodies far outnumber the soldiers. They are so numerous that our coats appear to be alive. Some of the officers found a manor house, and though it disappointed us for provisions, they brought back five bottles of brandy, which caused great cheer despite our miserable circumstances.

I think of you, my dear family, and wonder how you

are faring. I hope my little sisters and brothers are keeping up their studies and that you, my father, are kissing the grapes each day for me. I hope this will not be my last letter. The hope of reuniting with all of you keeps me alive.

Your loving son,

Rupert

Rupert's letter circulated among his family and friends. The Herr family draped their front door with black crepe. Life went on, but there were fewer and fewer young men at the festivals. We became a town of women, children, and old men. We received news from the front infrequently. Letters from our boys and rumors and gossip circulating among the townspeople supplied us with the only news we had.

The news was not good. Napoleon now seemed far from invincible. Supply lines between the front and the homeland seemed not to be functioning. He set his troops loose to scour the poor farms and fields for any food they could find. He marched the starving, lice- and disease-ridden men to exhaustion. As far as we could tell, troops were not paid, provisioned, or protected. Finally, in December, we received another letter. It had taken two months to reach us. The handwriting was barely legible.

October 1812

Dearest family,

Please forgive my bad writing, as I am writing this on the bare ground with hands that are stiff from being frozen. I cannot describe all the horrors I have seen. God has spared me through three battles, but yesterday, my right leg was shot through by a fleeing peasant. As we approached the Russian frontier, the people fled before us, and retreating Russian soldiers burned everything—farms, fields, and villages. They left no living creature that might assuage our intense hunger. Hunger and cold motivate our every action.

Most of my German brothers are dead. Those who did not die of their wounds have contracted typhus, spread by the armies of lice that infest our bodies. The few of us that remain care not for Napoleon nor the Russians nor any other people. We must all die of hunger soon. All has been burned. Moscow is a seven-hour walk from here, and rumors are flying that it too has been set afire.

Today my wound is aflame and oozing. I will not be marching to Moscow. I have given my woolen coat to a brother who still has a chance to survive. I understand that dying from cold is not too unpleasant. It certainly cannot be worse than hunger.

If God spares me, then I apologize for causing you undue concern. But if he does not, I wanted you to have my last confession of love.

Your loving son,

Rupert

We sat in stunned silence. They say that each person experiences grief in his or her own way. I believe that is only partly true. We shared the same pain, the same devastation, the same despair. Our grief was a common bond. We waited and waited but did not hear from him again. His name was posted on the church door as missing. The ache of not knowing, of wondering wore me down. I cried until I was wrung dry. He had disappeared along with all but a few of our young men.

Those few who survived trickled back. The young men who left our town now seemed old, taciturn, and greatly diminished by their trials. Of the seven thousand men of our province who were led away by Napoleon to the Russian frontier, only nine hundred returned. There were no words for our devastation. It was a communal suffering that affected everything—our homes, our schools, our church, our farms and businesses, our entire society. But worst of all, it hardened our hearts. A vicious cynicism, a feeling of having been victimized, infected our once-happy fatherland. It was time for the many provinces of German-speaking people to unite into one nation so we could defend our homeland. I did not realize when I recorded the events of Napoleon's war in my book of days that this goal was many decades from being fulfilled. But the sentiment was growing among us.

CHAPTER 6

THE LAND OF IN BETWEEN

1813–1814

I lived in the "land of in between." I was not young but not yet old—not a wife, mother, or hausfrau yet not quite the independent person my girlhood self had envisioned, neither fully accepted in my craft nor rejected. On the surface, despite our losses, life went on as before. Each day I threw open the shop's shutters and greeted the people in the street as I had done for five years, but with less optimism and enthusiasm. I measured, cut, sewed, seamed, and kept the books. But life had changed in unseen ways. We all carried scars—Mama inward scars from the death of another child, Francisca outward scars from the pox, Father from the loss of his only son, and I from the loss of my vivacious brother and my beloved Rupert.

Mama kept Francisca, eight years old after Napoleon's war, home from school for fear the other children would mock her. Father objected to this. I could hear them arguing in the evening after the lamps and candles were extinguished and the house was dark. Their muffled, disembodied voices, drifting through the walls, conveyed feelings hidden by the light of day.

"No child of mine will be an illiterate peasant," Father insisted to Mama.

"She's only eight. You have been reading to her for years, as I have taught her letters. You've seen Anastasia teaching her sums as she works on the bookkeeping. That should be enough. I don't think a girl needs to have a strong education," Mama retorted.

"Nonsense. This is a new age. Francisca will not be an ignorant mother for her children."

It was as if he had driven a spike through Mama's heart. He immediately regretted his words. Mama had only the most rudimentary education. Father's words implied that she was the prime example of ignorant motherhood.

Father immediately softened his tone. "You know what I mean, liebchen. Francisca faces an uncertain future. She will need all the benefits we can give her. Look at Anastasia—only seventeen, and she could almost run this business by herself if I passed away." My heart swelled hearing Father's praise.

Mama became silent for several long moments. Her voice was soft but firm. "I will not have the other schoolchildren scar her further with their cruel taunts."

In the end, Father relented. Father's collection of books doubled as texts to improve her reading skills. Francisca would not be ignorant, but her preparation to face the world would be stunted. She had always been shy, and staying home with us every day only made her more introverted. Mama would not take her out to the market. She did not play in the street with the other children. Her only contact with others was when she went to church with us as a family, where Mama hovered over her protectively.

Francisca proved an adept student in our homemade school. Though her skill with numbers was limited, she excelled at reading. Over time, Father's library had grown steadily, providing us a rich well from which we could draw. I carefully chose books that challenged her reading ability and expanded her horizons beyond the narrow borders of our town. Despite her enforced domesticity, Francisca's understanding and appreciation of the written word and her knowledge of the world grew far beyond her years. In some ways, her knowledge was deeper than that of her age-mates who had stayed in school but learned only what the meisters taught them.

During the summer, Mother put Francisca to work in our kitchen garden. She showed a talent with vegetables. She learned how to harvest her vegetables at the best moment, how to dry them or salt them so we could eat them during the long winter months. She even experimented with the new process of preserving vegetables by heating them in glass jars with rubber seals. When she was among her thriving plants, she bloomed like the bearded irises in spring.

Mama taught her to crochet. Her special gift to Francisca was to school her in tatting, making dainty, lacey frills with thread so thin and needles so small only the most skillful hands could manage it. These skills suited Francisca's long-fingered hands and made use of her talent for fine work.

Father, Francisca, and I all looked forward to visits from the bookseller. Old Herr Frankel, with his long, frizzled beard and black hat, traveled more extensively than anyone else in our community, far beyond the Schwarzwald that defined our universe. He had cleverly negotiated an agreement with the margrave, whose family was indebted to Abraham's family for loans that kept the margrave's family solvent. Letters of introduction from Karl Friedrich, margrave of the State of Baden, identified Abraham as the margrave's personal book buyer and gave him access to booksellers and publishers in university towns from Freiburg to Frankfurt and publishing centers from Strasburg to Leipzig. As a Jew, he was banned from the guilds, but this gave him freedom to roam. Though he was harassed or looked upon with suspicion in many towns, he also made many friends.

Garrulous old Herr Frankel talked to everyone, bringing back colorful descriptions of bustling markets, festivals, clothes, and customs in neighboring areas. In three small villages south of our town, the Protestant girls wore hats topped with eleven outsize red pom-poms. And in Strasburg, they wore ridiculously huge, black bows on their heads. We all laughed when he sketched pictures of these poor girls and their embarrassing head wear. But it was books he loved best. He had a sharp eye and an even sharper mind. For the margrave, he purchased expensive first editions. For his other readers, he kept a sharp eye out for used books, forgotten books, castoffs from estate sales of the privileged class. He sought out the newest ideas in philosophy, science, and politics. As an outsider, he viewed the world with a cynical insight.

He brought home terrifying details of the countryside leading into Leipzig. Napoleon's Grande Armee had crossed back and forth across this land, leaving devastation in its wake. Not only did the troops take chickens and potatoes but they scoured chests and cupboards for anything useful, set fire to thatched roofs, and murdered women and children in their mothers' arms. He described the ghosts of dismembered trees and the smell that clung to burned, abandoned villages. The roadside ditches beyond Eisenach were clogged with the bones of both dead horses and unknown soldiers from both sides of the conflict. I shuddered to think of our boys, sacrificed on the altar of Napoleon's ambition.

I was grateful our town had been spared the physical devastation of war, but we were not spared the grief of Napoleon's fiasco in Russia. Only a few of those who marched off to war that drizzly spring morning had returned. There were fewer young men to enliven our festivals and plough our fields. Nearly every family suffered the loss of their men and boys. In some cases, widows took over their husbands' businesses. Some farms had to rely on the labor of unrelated, itinerant ex-soldiers, outsiders who had no loyalty to our community, no love for our customs, and no respect for women and girls. We still believed in the ideals of the French Revolution—farmers should own the land they tilled, the ruler should be guided by the wishes and needs of the governed, those who showed ability and diligence should merit advancement—but we were bitterly disillusioned by the outcome of the revolution.

In our little town, however, our institutions continued as they had always been. The guilds remained strong, which, paradoxically, both protected and limited our craftsmen. We resumed our festivals, schools stayed open, the rulers remained in their castles, and life went on. But despite this outward veneer of normalcy, we could feel change in the air.

Now, at age seventeen, I had been the tailor's apprentice for two years. I accompanied Father to the fabric merchant and learned to detect subtle differences between bad, mediocre, good, and excellent cloth. I could create a paper pattern from the measurements Father gave me, wasting as little fabric as possible; sharpen the scissors to perfection; stitch flat-felled seams and blind hems; perfect buttonholes; and craft rounded shoulders without a single pucker. The only thing I was forbidden to do was apply the measuring tape to a man's torso. Father strictly forbade this intimacy.

When there were lulls in the day's work, I started redesigning the beautiful dress Father had given me for Christmas many years ago. Patiently, I picked apart the side seams, adding lively ribbons for color and a dark maroon border to the lower hem to accommodate a taller stature. Father showed me the delicate skills necessary to widen the shoulders and lengthen the sleeves.

Snow started falling early that year, making travel over frozen ground easier. As Christmas drew near, Father removed the wheels of the old cart and replaced them with the runners we used in winter. The horse pulled us over smooth, hard packed tracks unmarred by rough patches of exposed cobbles. Father, Francisca, and I tramped through Schultz's woodlot searching for the perfect Christmas tree, as Gilly and I had years before. Wet snow clung to our high, laced-up winter boots as we each set out in our own direction searching for the perfect tree.

"Eeek!"

Father and I came running when we heard Francisca's cry. We found her in a tree well.

"What happened to you?" I laughed.

Obviously, Francisca had not been out in the woods often enough. Everyone knew that soft, loose snow accumulated around the outer edges of the evergreens where snow shed from the branches. Inside the encircling drifts were well-protected pockets near the base of the tree with almost no snow. Francisca had tried to climb the encircling berms of snow, only to find herself trapped at the base of the tree.

"I was just getting under the branches to see if the trunk was nice and straight," she wailed. "Now I can't get out of here." Her arms were flailing and her face reddening.

Father and I stopped laughing when we saw how close she was to tears.

"It's all right. Don't worry. Stand as close to the tree trunk as you can." Father's authoritative voice immediately calmed her nerves. "I'll go get a rope." As Father returned to the cart, I began singing "Oh Tannenbaum." By the time he returned with the rope, both Francisca and I were singing and laughing.

"Now tie this around your waist and stretch out. Pretend you are swimming in the pond," Father instructed Francisca as he threw her the rope with a loop knotted around one end.

Francisca "swam" through the fluffy snow until she was back in the deep snow between the trees. When she emerged, shaken but not hurt, I gathered up a handful of snow and tossed it gently in her direction. She took the cue and returned fire. Soon we were scrambling around in knee-high snow engaged in a snowball battle. Father smiled indulgently, glad to see his daughters acting like children again.

We laughed and played in the snow, capturing a moment of happiness as fleeting as the snowflakes on our eyelashes. Francisca's mottled face brightened, and once more, I saw the face of a still-beautiful girl with a strong, serious soul.

Christmas was not as it had been, but we repeated the beloved rituals of the season. We hung small, red Christmas apples, specially purchased from the Alsatian vendors at the Christmas market; Mama's tatted snowflakes; and a small, clumsily decorated pinecone ornament made by Gilly when he was six. Francisca's face reflected the amber glow of the candles as she earnestly enacted the ritual of lighting the tree for the first time. Father topped the tree with the beautiful star Gilly and I had bought when we were still innocents.

I disappeared into the room I now shared with Francisca and emerged with a bundle.

"This is for you, Francisca." I offered her a package decorated with bows. I felt an odd mix of pride and anxiety, not knowing if my project would be a success.

"What is it?" Francisca was thunderstruck. Her face flushed with emotion as she untied the ribbon. She held the remade dress up against her body, just as I had once done. She wanted to race off to try it on at once, but Mama stopped her.

"I have something for you too, *mein mausi.*" Mama had begun calling Francisca her "little mouse" when she'd shown a propensity for digging in the garden dirt. Mama handed her a small, square package tied with the prettiest ribbon we had in the shop. I recognized it immediately. Francisca solemnly untied the ribbon.

"Thank you, Mama, but what will I do with this?" Francisca asked, gazing at her book of empty pages.

"Your heart needs a place to rest its troubles. This is a book of days. In it, you can write all your thoughts and feelings. It will be yours, and only yours, forever," Mama replied.

A sense of déjà vu surged through me as memories engulfed me.

Light from the candles danced over us as we joined hands around our tree. Mama's warbling soprano blended with Father's basso profundo, Francisca's perfectly pure, piercing high notes and my alto. Our voices resonated, strengthened by each other, a family of voices raised against our sorrows.

Francisca walked with her chin held high, almost as if she felt beautiful, as we shuffled through the street to midnight Mass, greeting our friends and neighbors. She held her head a little higher as she gripped Mama's hand.

One year ended harmoniously, and the next began hopefully. Inspired by the New Year, and aspiring to rejuvenate our spirits and our business, I began a new project. Working on Francisca's dress had given me an idea. Most women made clothing in their own homes for their families and themselves—serviceable overskirts and aprons for the women and loose-fitting trousers and jackets of a coarse cotton weave for the men. Some women took in piecework as seamstresses, repairing or altering clothing for others. The well-to-do burghers' wives sometimes ordered more elegant frocks from dressmakers in fashionable cities like Strasburg or Berlin, but no one I had ever known designed her own patterns, chosen fabric, and executed her own creations.

With Father's blessing, I began creating a beautiful new dress. Using the dress form I used for women's cloaks, I laid out a pattern that was simple and elegant but not ostentatious. It was an Empire-waisted gown in a pale eggshell color. I used *kattun* chintz fabric, a closely woven, plain cotton with a lustrous finish sold by traveling vendors from the province of Alsace. A double row of delicate ribbons cascaded down the front of the dress from the high waist to the hem. A deep maroon ribbon of rare silk, the same ribbon I had used for Francisca's dress, encircled the bodice and was tied in a simple bow at the front. The long sleeves were attractively puckered at the top, tapering to form a smooth forearm, coming to a point over the back of the hand. With great satisfaction, I draped a maroon-trimmed cloak over the shoulders of the form to complement the beautiful dress. I mounted it on a dress form and placed it prominently at the front of the shop so it was the first thing our customers saw when they entered.

I was at the stage of my craft when, if I had been a young man, I would apply for my "wander book" and undertake my journeyman's travels. For centuries, when experienced apprentices reached young adulthood, they donned journeyman clothing and, with journey book in hand, traveled near and far, working for masters in other cities. This is what Father had done. He fondly recalled his wander years and sometimes told us tales of his adventures as we sat before the fire on cold winter nights.

Journeymen enjoyed a camaraderie particular to young men their age. They suffered hardships and were sometimes caught out in the elements, hungry and homeless, but once they found a master to take them in, they enjoyed professional recognition and a status not given to mere apprentices. By working for master craftsmen in new cities, they mastered both their trade and the ways of the world outside their sheltered childhood homes. When their wander years were over, they could produce their masterpiece, qualify as a master craftsman, join the guild, settle down, and get married. It was not exactly an easy, carefree time, but despite its occasional hardships and privations, the young journeymen found adventure and friendship. They socialized with their age-mates, celebrating the arrival of new journeymen with raucous initiation parties.

Father's favorite city was Vienna. He had trekked over 350 miles, across rivers, mountains, and fields to reach this glamorous city. Having lived in Vienna gave him an aura of worldliness and culture. Along the way, he'd traveled through Stuttgart, Munich, and Salzburg, taking positions with prominent master tailors. But Vienna was his crowning achievement. It was huge, with over two hundred thousand inhabitants and was a major center of arts, music, and letters. His eyes took on a blurry glaze when he recalled that time of his life. His master, a man named Buchlieber, had a vast collection of over a thousand books. This was a testament to the culture of Vienna, as well as to the master's erudition, prosperity, and skill. His wealthy clients paid well but expected perfection. Father enjoyed shining times in Vienna.

One wintery evening, having heard about Herr Buchlieber for the fiftieth time, I ventured to ask a question that always puzzled me. "Why didn't you stay in Vienna? Why didn't you qualify as a master in that glorious city? Why did you ever come back here to our small town in the Schwarzwald?"

"Well, I loved Vienna, but Vienna did not love me. I was a lowly, small-town journeyman with no connections." He sighed.

"Then why did your master take you in the first place?" I wondered.

"You see, schatzele, it was for exactly that reason that he hired me. I was no threat to him or any of the other burghers. They knew I, a Roman Papist, would never be accepted by the Lutheran majority that controlled the guild. So I made my way back toward my homeland. But there was a silver lining." He raised his eyebrows and his eyes twinkled, looking toward Mama by the fireside, leaning over her darning.

"In Haigerloch, I met your mother," he crooned. "She was almost as tall as I, and elegant. I first noticed her in the market, basket looped over her arm, chatting with some other women. Wavy, honey-tinged brown hair flowed down her back, accentuating her slim waist. All her movements were graceful and contained. When she turned her handsome face toward me, her gray eyes locked me in place. She hustled away, eyes fixed on her footfalls. I immediately set about asking who she was." Father beamed.

Mama blushed, looked up, and returned his gaze. In her face, I saw traces of the graceful, serene young lady she once was. "He was so handsome in his journeyman outfit, black double-breasted vest, with eight bright silver buttons matching the six silver buttons on his black coat, belled pants, and tall black hat. My father, your grandfather, was a well-respected furniture maker. He made it difficult for any young man to approach me." Her voice trailed off.

"So true, so true." Father picked up the thread of the conversation. "It took me two years to win her heart, and Herr Stehle allowed us to marry only after I'd achieved master craftsman status."

The stories of Father's wander years left me with an uneasy, restless feeling. When I was sixteen, I had been so happy to be the tailor's apprentice. I'd never thought of what would happen later. Now, at eighteen, I was marooned on the island of perpetual apprenticeship, with well-developed skills but unable to sail on to the port of master craftsmanship. My mind twisted and turned, trying to invent a new path. I fantasized about donning the costume of a journeyman and trying to pass as a young man. But I was too small to look like anything but a twelve-year-old boy. In any case, I would not be allowed to enter other cities without a journey book as a passport, much less apply to work for a master craftsman. The guild would never permit such a terrible breach of tradition. Nor would Father ever agree to it. I hesitated to share my feelings, and when I did, Father didn't perceive my problem.

"I would love to travel and see the world. It's not fair that I am not allowed my travel book. I am just as qualified as any young male apprentice." My voice rose to a whine.

"But, schatzele, aren't you happy working here with me?" Father deflected my angst.

"Yes, of course I am, but I can never move forward. I will be your apprentice forever." I tried to make my feelings clear without insulting his generosity.

"You have already established yourself as a skilled schneider, and now you are making dresses! How many other girls do you know who have accomplished as much?"

I could hardly argue with him. Katy Herr, whose brothers never came back from the war, was wearing herself out helping with the most menial jobs in the shoemaker's shop and doing the housework her sickly mother could not do. Matilda Kohler's father had too many mouths to feed. Though they already had nine children, Matilda's mother gave birth to one more this year, when she should have been finished with her childbearing years. Then without Matilda's consent, she was married off to a cooper, a simple builder of barrels. The match was clearly beneath her. I understood Father's point but still felt the hollowness of unfulfilled ambition.

"Your originality and good-heartedness have contributed to our success. And what would Francisca do without you?" Father continued.

It was gratifying to hear his praise, but his last argument slammed the door in my face. Of course. How could I be so selfish? My family needed me right here, not wandering about the countryside. Though my restless heart longed to ramble and roam, my sex and my obligations tied me irrevocably to this place. "You're right. I could never leave Mama, Francisca, and you." I sighed and silently relegated my thwarted ambitions to the dark corner of my soul, where I stored my other losses.

I found my respite in books. Books took me to places I could not go. They stimulated my expanding view of the world and initiated me into the world of ideas and philosophy normally available only to the highly educated, elite boys in our famous universities.

As long as I did not neglect my responsibilities to the family business, Father never objected to seeing me hunkered in a corner with a book. Tutoring Francisca gave me plenty of excuses to explore the world of words. Just as Francisca's greatest joy was digging in the garden to bring forth new life, mine was strolling through the garden of gorgeous language and the netherworld of lofty thoughts.

I had a ravenous mind that feasted promiscuously on all types of books. I found treasures, like the unexpected joy of reading the poetry of the peasant woman, Anna Louisa Karsch; the intense, realistic dramas of Johann Wolfgang von Goethe; and the philosophy of Immanuel Kant, which I must admit I barely understood. The romances of Sophie von La Roche were a guilty pleasure. I had to hide them in my bed lest Father and Mama discover them. I learned about so many oddities, for example that, in 1726, a black African became professor of philosophy at the University of Halle and wrote enlightened tragedies. I had never laid eyes on an African man of any color. Yet there he was, introducing himself to me through his books. Through reading, I tried to quell the rebellion of my restless soul and discover peace in my unquiet heart.

CHAPTER 7

EXPECTATIONS

1822–1828

By 1822, Napoleon was a bad dream, left behind in the light of the new day. He was a storm that had passed over the horizon and then disappeared. Life went on as usual, and we were at peace.

The cycle of annual festivals replayed itself as it had for centuries. A few days before our annual Lenten fast began, we celebrated the Fasnacht Festival. Seventeen-year-old Francisca surprised all of us by expressing a desire to participate. The pre-Lenten festivities were meant to bid winter goodbye and celebrate the joyful anticipation of spring. They gave us all a chance to uncork emotions bottled up by winter's confinement. Costumed friends and neighbors marched the streets in wooden masks depicting witches and the evil spirits of winter—images so old no one even remembered their origins. The disguises gave us freedom from social restrictions and allowed behaviors that would otherwise have been forbidden.

This year, I set to work constructing a complicated costume of disk-shaped fabric patches arranged in an overlapping scalelike pattern. Though this type of costume was normally loose fitting, I gave it a slim waistline, broad skirts, and tight bustline to complement Francisca's comely figure. Next, we borrowed a smiling, wooden mask from the Schultz girls.

Shrove Tuesday, the evening of the early spring festival parade, was nippy but clear and calm. We spectators could hear the marching band long before we saw the approaching torchlight. Witches with gruesome masks swished the streets with their brooms, driving away winter's demons. The layered fabric-patch costume warmed Francisca, but it was the mask that

71

liberated her. As she slipped into the boisterous crowd marching down the street, her spirit floated free. She danced and cavorted, twirling until her broad skirt flared, exposing her shapely ankles and calves. The young men took notice. Being in disguise encouraged pranksters. A group of young men surrounded the young women marching with Francisca's group. A few of them playfully rounded them up, while two or three boys crawled through the milling girls and tied their ankles together with twine. There was much tussling, falling and laughing as the girls worked to free themselves, while the boys tried to thwart their efforts.

As I watched from the sidelines, my heart swelled with joy for my sister, who had enjoyed very little attention from the young men of our town. I remembered my own time as a girl experiencing the pure intensity of young love. *Dear, lost Rupert. What might our life together have been?* I sighed. But such thoughts were of no use to me now. I was a mature twenty-five-year-old woman, almost approaching spinsterhood, with skills and responsibilities. A seed of hope still lived in my heart, waiting for warm sun to bring it to life. I tried to keep my heart open to whatever lay ahead.

After the parade had passed, the crowd returned to the square to find the freshly tapped barrels of *doppelbock*, a hearty quaff originally brewed by monks to sustain them during Lenten fast, before Napoleon destroyed their monasteries. Today it would sustain us, as would the fat bratwurst now soaking in tubs of beer and butter, deep-fried sugared *krapfen* doughnuts, and spiced wine—all intended to fill our bellies before the forty-day fast began.

The smile I wore turned to an expression of dismay when I literally bumped into Matilda Kohler, now Matilda Stein. Three little children clung to her. A girl of about five gripped her skirt; a boy of three perched on her left hip; and a baby, perhaps six months old, rode in the sling across her breast.

"Matilda! Look at you! You're a"—my voice faltered—"a mother." Not knowing what to say, I couldn't stop from stating the obvious. She looked worn out, older than her twenty-five years. Her waist had thickened. Her skirts were frayed at the hem.

"You're a genius, Anastasia!" she laughed. "Always the smartest one."

"How *are* you?" I blubbered.

"Well, as you can see, I'm quite busy. Our little house above the barrel shop is crowded. Klaus, my husband, is good-hearted but not a good businessman. So we struggle a bit. But he is loving; kind to the children; and, best of all, funny. Though we are not prosperous like your father, we keep ourselves fed, and we laugh a lot. We sometimes lack new clothes, but we never lack love." When she smiled, I could hear that my dear Matilda still had her wickedly funny sense of humor. Though she'd married young and seemed destined to bear many children, life had not yet scrubbed the patina of good humor off her.

I tried to hug her, but the children attached to her every surface prevented me. I gently squeezed her arm and wished her well, imagining, once again, what my life might have been like if I had married Rupert.

We said our goodbyes and went our separate ways. A little nostalgia embedded itself in my heart. I told myself that I could not stand in the same river that had flowed back in our schoolgirl days. The stream had flowed onward. There was a new river in which to bathe, and it was changing every day.

Torches blazed. As the evening grew cooler, heavy woolen sweaters and overcoats rubbed against each other as we ate at the long tables set up around the bandstand. Voices rang out as we sang along to our favorite polkas, schottisches, and waltzes. Dancers from five to seventy-five crowded the open space in front of the band. As the night progressed, laughter grew louder and more raucous. It was time for me to leave the festivities.

I strolled through the streets heading for home. On a corner near the square was a group of burghers talking jovially to a man I had never seen before. He was tall and straight of spine, with a square jaw and a pronounced cleft chin, just like Father's. His worsted wool suit and well-tailored, pale gray cloak of fine merino sheep's wool told me he had good taste and a good income. He quickly looked over his shoulder as I passed, and for a moment, his expression changed from mirth to attentiveness. Then, just as quickly, he returned to his conversation.

The forty days of repentance and fasting ended, and the buds of early spring had burst into small, teal green leaves. A glorious Easter Sunday began with the peal of church bells that had hung silently in the belfry since Good Friday, as a sign of mourning. I snatched one of the pussy willow branches decorating our window box for each of us. We brought them to the church with us to be blessed.

CINDY MAYNARD

The dark, winding stairs to the choir loft smelled earthier than they had during winter when all smells were cleansed by the cold air. The rich, mellow harmonies of our adult choir floated out over the congregation. Men's and women's voices blended to express the eternal dawning of the season of hope. We sang Handel's solemn High Mass, topped off by an inspiring performance of the *Messiah*. As I left church, I saw the handsome stranger walking with Herr Krueger, the clock maker.

"Who is he?" I asked Father. Father knew nearly everyone coming or going from town.

"That's Herr Matthias Kist," he whispered. "He's the son of a clock maker from Neusatz." His tone was matter-of-fact. He glanced at me with one eyebrow lifted. "Why do you ask?"

I felt a hum, a buzz, a soft stir beginning inside me. "I suppose it's just the novelty of seeing a new face," I told both Father and myself.

Neither of us believed me.

Spring was glorious. A sense of anticipation spread through the family. Last year, Francisca had harvested the seeds from her strongest, tastiest vegetables and stored them in the dark, cool cellar. This year, she expected to grow the best garden she had ever grown. Peace brought prosperity, attracting more women to the shop looking for my custom-tailored dresses. Mama finally seemed more even-keeled as the losses of her children receded into the past. Father was getting older. The knuckles on his fingers were knobby and bulbous. His eyes were almost useless from a lifetime of close work. The fine work now fell to me. He still measured inseams and visited the fabric markets, where he was as well liked and respected as ever.

One fragrant morning as I flung open the shutters, the bell over the front door rang, giving me no time to compose myself. The first customer to walk into the shop was the clock maker's son from Neusatz. Close up, he seemed taller. I reached only to his chin and had to look up into his startling blue eyes. He stood a little closer to me than was necessary, but I didn't back away. My stomach churned, though I was not hungry. His face was impassive as his eyes scanned mine intently.

"Guten Morgen, Herr ..." I trailed off.

"Herr Kist," he informed me.

"Good morning, Herr Kist. How may I help you?" I practiced my most charming smile with good effect. I could see his demeanor softening.

"I'm looking for the master schneider. I was told this was his shop."

"Yes, that's my father, Herr Burkart. I'd be happy to call him. I believe he is still upstairs. But maybe I can help you?"

He looked confused. He was not from our town and did not take my presence in the tailor shop for granted as the other townspeople now did. I smiled a little wider, enjoying the surprised look on his face. I couldn't help straightening and throwing my shoulders back. I felt like a teenager trying to prove myself. "I'm the tailor's assistant. I have been his apprentice for many years and now serve nearly all our customers' needs." My declaration had a defensiveness I had not intended.

His eyes widened and he struggled a bit to maintain his composure. "Really? And he allows this?" It was hard to read his reaction. His face belied a mixture of bemusement and disdain.

"Why yes. I can do almost any tailoring task our customers require." I didn't really think he wanted to know my qualifications, so I dropped the subject. My heart was pounding, animated by an unknown energy. I felt confused by my emotions. Somehow, it seemed he was both patronizing and interested in me. Yet he paid closer attention to me than anyone had since Rupert.

"I'll go get him." I conceded defeat.

"Guten Morgen, Herr Kist." Father descended the stairs unsteadily, leaning on the half-timbered walls for support.

It was Herr Kist's turn to be flustered, as though he had been caught in a compromising situation. "I was just looking for someone to make a simple vest for me. The fabric of this one is becoming frayed." He pulled aside his frock coat to demonstrate. He had a trim waist and broad shoulders. He was more muscular than a clock maker needed to be.

"Anastasia, I am not feeling well this morning. My arthritis is flaring up. Would you please take the measurements?" Father then dismissed himself and hoisted himself back up the stairs.

"Of course." I tried to seem matter-of-fact, but I felt far from normal. Father had recently allowed me to take upper body measurements of older, well-known men customers, but this was the first time I had laid my hands upon a strange man.

"Please remove your coat," I tried to sound authoritative but respectful. He removed his coat in stunned silence and submitted to my ministrations. I worked methodically, refusing to look into his eyes, and concentrated on the fine details of the measurements, making sure they were precise. He shifted his weight from foot to foot and breathed deeply. Was he as nervous as I? If he was, he wasn't having much success concealing it. I smiled inwardly and relaxed into my work.

"What brings you to our town?" I tried to break the tension with small talk.

"I've been speaking to Herr Krueger about taking me on. I've completed my journeyman years and want to create my master work." His chest swelled a bit, just as I was measuring it.

So, pride is what nourishes you, I thought, as I remeasured his chest. "Herr Krueger is an excellent craftsman. I'm sure you will enjoy working with him."

Herr Krueger was indeed an excellent clock maker. He had a demeanor almost as imperious as Herr Kist's. I considered him prideful, though others praised him for his strength of character.

After I had finished measuring Herr Kist's broad chest, I lifted my head abruptly. My head struck his chin sharply. He had been looking down at me the entire time I worked.

"Oh my goodness. I'm so sorry," I blubbered as I rubbed the crown of my head.

"No need to be sorry. It's nothing."

As he rubbed his chin, our eyes met again. We both smiled and then laughed. What were we laughing about? It didn't matter. I knew at that moment I would see him again.

Herr Krueger accepted Matthias Kist under his tutelage. I seemed to see Matthias everywhere I went—in the market, at the bakery. I even tried to think of a reason I needed to visit the clock shop. The townspeople, always curious about a new face in town, had learned more about Matthias, and gossip circulated through the market. He was, in fact, the son of a clock maker. When his father had died, Matthias had been too young to take over the business. The guild had installed Herr Berthold Kraus in his father's shop. Matthias's mother had soon married the new clock maker, as often happened. Suddenly Matthias had a new stepfather and was relegated to second place in his mother's heart.

Mama and Father were not blind to my interest in Matthias, whose wardrobe was apparently falling apart. He found reasons to require my services at every opportunity. On one occasion, I found shirt seams that had been deliberately opened so they would require repair. In July, my parents invited him for Sunday dinner with the family. So, with the blessings of my family, I began keeping company with Matthias.

Our favorite pastime was walking the rocky forest paths through deep woods and friendlier byways through vineyards and orchards. After a time, we ventured farther into the darkness of the deep forest. Whether she liked it or not, Francisca always accompanied us as chaperone. It would be unseemly for us to be walking alone together, and neither Mama nor Father had strength for long rambles in the hills. She appeared not to like it at all and wandered off to inspect the growing things in "God's garden" as she called the lush green Schwarzwald. Our little mausi often had her nose poked under bushes or between rocks, like the little scurrying creatures that were her namesake, leaving Matthias and I alone for private conversation. There was a magnetism between Matthias and me that made it difficult not to follow nature's course. I was shocked that my body responded to his in ways that were both delicious and frightening.

Matthias became a regular at our Sunday dinner table. Conversations between Father and Matthias were disconcerting. Matthias shared very few of Father's "enlightened" ideas. Despite his acceptance of my workmanship, he could not conceal his disapproval of my working. I chose to overlook his staid attitudes. I thought he would get used to the idea over time. In any case, if I married, everyone assumed I would need to give up my independent work anyway. It was one thing to take over an existing business when a husband died or a father failed to a return from war. In those cases, the widow assumed responsibility until a son or apprentice was ready to take over. Her tenure in the business was like that of a regent queen, waiting for the heir apparent to mature into the kingship. But it was quite another matter for a woman to work if her husband could support the family with his craft.

We did not speak of this. Matthias harbored no doubts about his place in the world or his future wife's place in the family. He fully expected to be the unquestioned head of the household, whose wife would conform to strict social norms. None of this seemed to matter to me. It was as if my lifelong desire to float my own boat had sunk beneath the relentless tides of desire.

After Rupert's death, I did not make long-range plans. I lived each day as it came, secure in my skills. I did not worry about finding a husband, so I never considered what would become of my relative independence if I ever married. Marriage seemed a remote possibility. I assumed I would always make my own way in the world, as I had envisioned when I was a young girl. The unexpected arrival of Matthias had ignited a firestorm of conflict in me. I loved my work. I prided myself on my skill and ingenuity. A large part of my inward picture of myself was constructed of fabric, thread, and scissors. Throwing open the shutters at dawn and working the ledgers in lamplight at dusk bounded my days with a sense of security and self-assurance. I simply ignored the consequences of how marriage would tear that construction apart or slam those shutters closed forever.

"I love nothing better than a good sauerbraten. My mother's recipe is a family heirloom," Matthias said at one of our Sunday dinners. He smiled ingratiatingly at Mama as she brought the aromatic stew to the table to join the small mountain of steaming boiled red potatoes from Francisca's garden.

"I'm sure Anastasia's will be equally delicious." Mama modestly lowered her gaze. Her cheeks colored a bit. She was not accustomed to compliments.

"Is Anastasia as good a cook as you are?" Matthias kept up the friendly banter.

"Oh no," she cooed. "Anastasia is busy in the shop or keeping the books or practicing with the choir. She spends very little time in the kitchen," said Mama, innocent of the reaction this would provoke in Matthias.

"Oh well, I'm sure she can learn," Father put in. "She is very bright. She is very well-read, you know," he added with no small measure of pride. "She has read Johann Wolfgang von Goethe and Friedrich von Schiller and is well informed by the gazettes."

"Oh really?" Matthias's back straightened a bit as his voice lowered and his tone chilled.

"Oh, I'm sure I can learn. But I'll never be as good a cook as Mama." I wanted to explain that, from a very early age, I had known I would be bored to death by cooking and housework. But I thought it would be the wrong thing to say. Anyway, I thought, I will just need to change my ways when I become a wife. My stomach churned with anxiety.

That winter, Matthias and I skated on the pond, our hands joined as our arms crisscrossed in front of our bodies forming a kind of figure eight. He bent to untie the laces that secured the blades to my boots, just as Rupert had. He held every door open for me. The younger girls tittered as they skated past us, and the young boys shoved each other as they glided by, trying to distract us. But we remained in the cocoon of sparks that enveloped us as soon as we were near each other. I had often envied the courting couples, gliding in circles on the mill pond, gazing into each other's eyes. Now, I proudly glided over the ice, sure I was the envy of all, holding hands with my tall, elegant Matthias.

By the following spring, it was assumed we would be married. Though he did not formally propose or ask my father's permission to marry, we carried on as though it was a foregone conclusion. Francisca became less and less interested in supervising us, leaving us on our own for hours.

Marriage was a complicated transaction. The husband must be in a position to support a family. Most men needed to wait until they had produced their master work, been accepted into the guild, and found a town to accept them. Many young couples waited years before their union could be solemnized. Depending on the longevity of a town's master craftsman and the demand for the man's craft, men were often in their late thirties or even forties before they wed. In fact, my own beloved Father had been forty years old when he'd married Mama. And I had been born many months before the wedding officially took place. Although the birth of children to couples who intended to marry but were not yet able to do so was decried as sinful by the priests, the young couple was not usually shunned by the community if it was understood that they would be married at the first opportunity.

The August heat kindled our own personal fire, and our instincts got the best of us. Our kisses grew more ardent and prolonged. Our hands became fearless explorers, as if they had a quest of their own that they must fulfill. I discovered a molten core of passion I'd never before suspected. The sleeping volcano inside me boiled over. My passion was like a force of nature, unstoppable and unquenchable.

79

Nature took its course, and in November I had the inevitable conversation with Mama and Father. Mama cried. Father became stern and was very disappointed. Complex feelings—losing their daughter, losing a business partner, losing a companion—clouded their happiness at being grandparents at long last. Father had a visceral protective reaction. Mother intuitively wondered if Matthias would make me happy. Both of them were apprehensive about his intentions. After all, he had never actually asked for my hand. After the shock wore off a bit, Father became enraged. I saw a passion I had never suspected in Father as he stomped around the kitchen smashing his fist into the kitchen table.

"You know, Anton, you should not be so hard on them. Anastasia was already fourteen months old when we were married," Mama reminded him.

"I know!" Father shouted. "But I had already submitted my master work and was ready to become a master craftsman! Matthias is not ready to become a master. His future is very unclear. Will he even find a town who can take another clock maker?"

"Don't worry. They will find their way in the world together. It's time Anastasia finds a husband. She is not so young, you know," she countered.

She was right. I would soon be twenty-seven years old. Though I had seldom thought about my age, twenty-seven suddenly seemed ancient to me.

"Yes, I know, but Anastasia was always such a good girl. I never expected her to fall like this. I must have a serious conversation with Matthias." Father resolved to hold Matthias's feet to the fire.

Francisca, Mama, and I started to make wedding arrangements. I designed my own wedding dress. Mama knitted the warmest blankets and added a tatted ribbon to our family's heirloom baptismal gown. Francisca decided to plant flowers that would bloom in time for a spring wedding.

Peter Paul came into the world in June of 1823, demanding and wailing. Mama and Father were delighted. All their misgiving melted away like the winter snow when they held their newborn grandson.

Matthias was pleased by his son but maintained a distance. He seemed preoccupied. His distance extended to me as well. He had been ambiguous when Father spoke to him about marriage, strongly implying that, yes, there would be a wedding but refusing to commit to a formal marriage proposal or a date.

We continued to eat Sunday dinners together, go to church together, and keep company in full view of the townspeople. Young couples with babies but without the blessing of the Church were becoming a more and more common sight. Towns were growing more crowded. Journeymen returning from their journey years had trouble finding positions. The guild tried to maintain strict control over the number and types of master craftsmen allowed in each town, but increased pressure from skilled, unemployed, semipermanent journeymen craftsmen was taking its toll. In some towns, shoemakers, barrel makers, and blacksmiths were hanging out their shingles without the cooperation or permission of the guild. This created an overabundance of some crafts. Formerly respectable crafts that had provided modest but reliable income for a family were now not producing enough income to support a family.

I carried on as Father's apprentice and partner has I always had, strong in my faith that Matthias would soon become a master and find a suitable position. And so we waited, in a kind of limbo, behaving like a couple but not sharing a home and without the blessing of the Church. Older townsfolk avoided me, tut-tutting as I walked past on the street, baby in my arms. Some of the older ladies stopped asking me to design their dresses. Father made excuses and apologies for me at the guild meetings, but he always assured the burghers that the sacrament sanctifying our union was coming soon.

Choir continued to be my one opportunity to be with longtime friends, pursuing a shared love of the music. But there were raised eyebrows as time passed and they did not receive wedding invitations. To avoid controversy, I took a hiatus from choir. I did not want to allow my shame to tarnish the reputation of the choir. I could always return when things were put right, I thought.

When Peter Paul was three years old, I thought enough time had passed for the townspeople to accept my situation and no longer think of it as scandalous. I made my application to return to the choir. I fully expected to be welcomed back by choir members and choirmaster alike. But Meister Sanger, the choir director, was uncharacteristically distant.

"What will you do now, Anastasia?" Meister Sanger asked me when I made my intention to return clear.

"What do you mean? I would like to be an alto in the choir and start singing with the group again."

"No, no. That's not what I mean." Meister Sanger frowned.

Confusion engulfed me. I stared blankly at him.

"Haven't you heard? The clock maker, Meister Krueger, is looking for a new journeyman."

A bolt of lightning shot through me. My stomach shriveled into a hard knot. "What? No! Matthias is his journeyman. We are going to be married!" My alto voice soared to high soprano.

"Really? When was the last time you saw your Herr Kist?" Herr Sanger spoke low and slow like a rumbling thundercloud.

"He returned to Neusatz to visit his mother and step-father. He has been gone for about three months, but his is coming back soon." My voice was now positively shrill.

"Yes, three months is a long time for a visit, don't you think?" One eyebrow raised, his lips barely concealed a smirk.

"I don't know. What you are trying to say?" I staunchly refused to believe his implication.

"Meister Krueger and Matthias had a falling out. Herr Krueger called Matthias a stuck-up poser, with no real interest in learning what he had to teach." Herr Sanger continued, unrelenting. "Your Matthias has been talking to Meister Kraus the clockmaker in Neusatz." Herr Sanger sounded almost gleeful telling me the gossip. "I hear he is interested in expanding his business into Baden-Baden. Herr Reinbold, the wealthy banker, is investing in this project."

My face grew red. I had difficulty breathing. I turned without a word and flew down the old spiral stone stairs. It could not be true. I heard a few of my "friends" tittering as I stumbled out the door. I could not face my family. I sat by myself in the back row of St. Michael's Church. The darkened vault hid my eyes, on fire with burning tears. My chest caved in as if from a hard blow. The familiar sounds of the choir in the loft rolled over me, like storm clouds ahead of a torrent.

Finally, I dragged myself home. I bent over Peter Paul's little pallet lying at foot of my bed and gasped for air as I searched his face for any sign of the truth. The next day I wrote a long letter to Matthias:

My dearest Matthias,

I hope you are well. It seems like years since you've been here with me. Has it already been over three months? I miss you bitterly. It's been so long, and your visits have been so infrequent that our precious Peter Paul will not know you when you return. He has stopped asking when Papa will come home. He is talking like a little professor now and asks for stories every night before he will sleep. He loves you and misses you.

I have been searching my heart. I was sure it held the secret memory of the first time you told me you loved me. But after searching all through the sleepless night, I realized that you have never said those words to me. Do you love me, my dearest? I have given you every bit of my heart and body. There is an empty space in my soul that only you can fill.

When will you come home to me?

Yours,

Anastasia

It sounded so desperate and shameless. I didn't care. My pride was injured. I began to feel the earth slide from beneath my feet, as a bare hillside slides after a hard rain. I made my way to the post station on the road to Neusatz and consigned my letter to the next post rider headed in that direction.

Posted letters took days, sometimes weeks to deliver, depending on road conditions. Post stations along the roads served as overnight accommodations for travelers, way stations where exhausted carriage horses could be exchanged for fresh ones and blacksmith shops that repaired horseshoes or wagon wheels. It was a slow process that was usually, but not always, reliable. You could never be certain your letter reached its intended destination.

When I didn't hear from Matthias for two more months, I wrote again, sure that my letter had not arrived in Neusatz. This time, my tone was more terse, less pleading and heartsick. Finally, after six months, I heard back from Matthias. He made no reference to my letters. He simply announced that he would be back in June. It was 1827. Our baby was already four years old. One morning in July, the bell at the front door jingled, and in strode Matthias Kist, as tall, erect, and well-dressed as ever. I was paralyzed by confusion.

"You're here!" It was a stupid thing to say, but the words just slipped out of my mouth.

"I told you I was coming." He sounded a bit defensive.

"It has been so long! Why did you stay away so long?" I couldn't control my whining tone.

"Don't be so dramatic," he scolded. "I had family business to attend to." He would be no more specific than that.

This conversation was nothing like the reunion I had imagined for so many months. He did not sweep me up into his arms, apologize for his long absence, and kiss me as if he was dying of thirst and I was his desert oasis.

"Won't you get me some kaffee? I could use some of your Mama's pfeffernuss cookies." He smiled as he took the one upholstered seat in the shop, the one reserved for our best clients. He unfolded his long legs, leaned back, and smiled as if nothing in the world troubled him, as if he had never been gone. He had the air of a reigning monarch expecting to be served.

"There you are! I thought I recognized your voice from upstairs." Mama teetered unevenly down the steep stairs from above.

"Please come up and have some kaffee." She beamed at him.

"Now there's the way a good woman greets a man." He winked at me as he disappeared up the stairs with Mama, while I stood there like a discarded scrap of linen. I closed the shutters, latched the front door, and trudged up the stairs to our rooms above.

Peter Paul came from the bedroom we shared into the kitchen, clutching Gilly's old Kasperle mask. "Can I have some cookies too, Oma?" he asked, paying no attention to his father.

"Aren't you going to say hello to your papa?" I asked as I mounted the last stair.

"My papa?" Peter Paul looked between Matthias and Father, who had emerged from his bedroom.

"Don't you remember your papa?" I asked.

"Isn't Grandpa my papa?" He had had started calling Father Papa about two months after Matthias left. No one had corrected him.

"No, this is your papa. He was away on business for a while. But he's home now." I tried to keep my voice even and cheerful.

"You are his papa, aren't you!" I said as I turned my face to Matthias. It was less a question than an accusation.

"Yes, well, we'll have time to talk about that later." He dismissed the subject with a wave of his hand.

My aging father, now seventy-one, was less welcoming when he emerged from his room, awakened from one of his frequent afternoon naps. Decades of close work in poor light had begun to cloud his vision, but he could see clearly enough that Matthias was harboring a secret he was reluctant to divulge.

"Well, hello, Herr Kist," Father intoned with an air of formality.

"Delighted to see you again, Herr Burkart." Matthias stood and extended his hand, assuming the demeanor of a respectable, young professional.

"Really. And what family business were you attending to?" Father refused his proffered handshake. He did not hesitate to dive into the heart of the matter.

"Can't we have a little kaffee first?" Matthias tried to lighten the atmosphere.

"We expected to see you a year ago. You have not sent any word to us. You've left Anastasia to raise a fatherless boy." He plunged straight into the battle with righteous indignation.

"Well, you see, I needed to find another position with a different clock maker." Matthias was treading lightly, trying not to be snagged by the thorns in Father's words.

"So we heard. I understood you had bitter words with Herr Krueger." I had never seen Father on the offensive in this way. He took no quarter.

"Yes, well, his skills were not the best, and I felt I needed a more proficient meister to sponsor me." Matthias pursed his lips, like a fastidious old nun.

"Really? Well, I guess there are always two sides to a story. Though that's not quite what I heard." Father was not appeased but was willing to drop the subject.

"Yes, the master clock maker in Neusatz, my stepfather as you might recall, specializes in the most exquisite mechanical cuckoo clocks. Have you heard of them?" Matthias brightened as he answered.

"Yes, I have. It's a temporary fancy. It will soon pass." Father mumbled, unconvinced of the durability of this passing trend.

"No, I don't think so. And Meister Kraus wishes to expand his business into Baden-Baden. It's a wonderful opportunity." Matthias twittered as though this explained everything—the lack of communication, the abandonment, the shame.

"Well, let me ask you then, will there be a house for Anastasia and the boy in Baden-Baden? When will you take them with you? Will you bring them with you when you return from your visit here?" Father nearly spit out his words.

"No, I'm now staying with Meister Kraus and my mother at my family home. It is very small and crowded, but I will be ready for my guild exams very soon. I'm working on my masterwork now. It won't be too long." He held out a ray of hope.

Finally, Father softened a bit. "Well, you are here now. How long do you plan to stay?"

"I will be visiting only a short while. I just wanted to tell you in person about my new situation." Matthias was trying to redeem himself in Father's eyes.

And that was that. Father, generous as usual, made room in our house for the prodigal son. Matthias stayed with our family for a week. He did not help with any chores. He ate our food, drank our beer, and expected to be catered to. Mother doted on him. Peter Paul eyed him warily, and Matthias responded to him with perfunctory, wooden attempts at affection. I remained at home while Matthias spent his evenings at the tavern catching up with his former acquaintances.

On those evenings, when he was at the tavern, I lay in my bed, listening to Francisca's measured breathing and Peter Paul's restless squirming on his pallet on the floor. One night, when Matthias returned from the tavern, I crept out of my bed and into Matthias' room. Matthias was silhouetted against the windowpanes, the moonlight in his face. He turned to me and held out his arms. Wordlessly, I padded toward his strong embrace, buried my face in his broad chest, and breathed deeply. I didn't need his words. I needed him, his physical presence, his heaviness as he arched above me in the moonlight, his exhausted collapse when he was spent. He fell asleep almost at once. I took that small piece of him back to my room, propped myself up in the corner where the old walls came unevenly together, and cried until I fell asleep. Not a word was spoken between us.

In the morning, it was as if nothing had happened. Matthias announced he was returning to Neusatz but promised he would write soon. We all gathered at the front door to wave goodbye to him. Father was the first to turn away, mumbling something about, "I will be surprised if we ever see him again."

We did hear from him again, about one month later. He sent a wedding announcement with no letter, no explanation:

> Genoveva Reinbold and Anton Reinbold are proud to announce the marriage of their daughter, Elisabetha Reinbold, age twenty-seven, to Matthias Kist, age forty-three of Neusatz.

I felt like I had been slapped in the face. Even Father and Mama looked at me with pity. I didn't dare stare into my future. I was unmarried, with an illegitimate child and no prospective husband. I had been abandoned, replaced by another—fat, conventional daughter who happened to be the daughter of the banker who was financing the new clock shop in Baden-Baden. At least, that's how I imagined her. She would be happy to stand over tubs of laundry, cook, clean, make babies and a wonderful sauerbraten. She would never question his authority. She would never give him the pleasure I had given him. But their shared pleasure, whatever it would be, was at least blessed by the Church and the community. I had ruined my chances at happiness. Why had I let hope transform me into a gullible, lustful wench?

Two months later, my humiliation was complete. I fell headlong into despair. This time, before I missed my first monthly cycle, I knew immediately what had taken root in me. I knew Matthias had left me with this last remnant of himself the very same month he married Elisabetha Reinbold, the banker's daughter. He had known when he was here that he intended to marry her and abandon me. He had probably known many months before his visit. He had known when he'd enveloped me in his arms that last time that he would never marry me. He had known, but he had not had the courage to say. He had used me one last time and then was done with me forever.

This time, the baby was obvious to Mama within four months. She took me aside as she explained that the first child was conceived with the expectation that Matthias would marry me. This second child, born nine months after his marriage to Elisabetha, would not be so easily accepted by our community.

"You know, Anastasia, this child will bring shame on all of us." Her tone was even. She did not even try to lecture or inflict moral rectitude on me.

"I know, Mother." I looked at my shoes, the floor, and my soiled apron. I could not meet her eyes.

"I will write to my sister, Rosina in Offenburg," mama said softly, "It is a larger town. No one will know you there. My sister will know what to do with you."

For another two months, I worked as I always had. I wore loose-fitting clothing. People believed I was getting fat. At least that's what I hoped they believed. Luckily, there were cloth merchants in Offenburg, so I had a plausible reason to travel there.

My Aunt Rosina tolerated my presence. She was neither sympathetic nor judgmental. We did not know each other well, and she made no attempt to befriend me. I was thirty-one years old, old enough to know better, old enough to know exactly what I was doing.

The road to Offenburg was muddy and rutted. The winter's snow had barely disappeared when April rains began. The jostling of the farmer's cart was brutal. About a week after I arrived the bleeding started, two months too early. Aunt Rosina looked at me dispassionately.

"Aren't you going to call the midwife?" I panted and hissed through my pains, swearing I would not cry out.

"Why bother? This baby cannot live. It is much too soon."

Aunt Rosina left me to labor in a cold, dark attic room. I labored in solitude for ten hours. I bled profusely. Aunt Rosina checked on me every hour or so, making sure I was not dying. When it became clear the time was near, she mutely stayed at my side. Finally, a little form burst forth into the world. He was perfectly made. Every little nail on each tiny finger and toe was exquisite. He did not cry. He struggled to breathe. The chord was wrapped around his neck. I struggled through my pain to free him from its grip, but its tangled mass would not loosen. His strangled attempts to breathe finally stopped. His lips and tiny finger nails were tinged a bluish color. He opened an eye just enough for a sliver of cloudy gray to meet my eye, just enough to show me he knew and loved me, but he could not stay. His eyes closed. His perfect, tiny body turned cold. I baptized him myself, as parents are allowed to do in emergencies.

"I baptize thee, Alouysius Burkart, in the name of the Father, the Son, and the Holy Spirit. Born this day April 9, 1828, died April 9, 1828. You lived upon this earth for one half hour. God took you back to his bosom. May God go with you, my baby."

I lay back on my bloody sheets and wept. I wept for my lost lovers. I wept for my terrible weakness. I wept for myself. I wept for my baby.

At last, tenderness stirred in Aunt Rosina's heart. She gently took the tiny, cold body, no longer occupied by a soul and wrapped him up in a little bundle. I never saw him again. But I never forgot that one profound moment when his eye met mine. As short as our time together was, my soul bonded to his for eternity.

CHAPTER 8

CHANGING TIMES

1830–1831

It was the autumn of 1830. It was late fall. The grape harvest was at its busiest, filling the air with heady scents. The children of the town were back at school. Peter Paul had grown into a stalwart child. He was tall, like his father, Matthias Kist. But he was sturdier, square-jawed, and serious, like Mama. He inherited almost none of his features from me, except his hazel eyes.

When he heard the front door slam and Peter crying, Father came teetering down the steep stairs. Father was now seventy-three. Rheumatism made his descent precarious. He pressed a hand firmly against the half-timbered wall to steady himself, and he concentrated on every step. It was unusual for Peter Paul, now seven, to cry.

I was attending to Frau Herzen, conferring about the design of a wedding dress for her daughter, Gertrude. Father reached the sniveling boy before I did.

"Peter, your nose is bleeding! What on earth happened to you?" Father was genuinely surprised. "Let's get you upstairs so you don't disturb Frau Herzen."

"It's all right, Anastasia. We can continue our discussion another time. You go now and see about your boy." The good Frau Herzen left the shop.

I hurried upstairs to our living quarters. "Peter!" I spit out, as I bustled to the washbasin with a handful of Peter's collar gripped in my fist. "We've got to get you cleaned up." He squirmed and flinched as I sluiced away the blood that was already starting to clot.

"Your nose is a mess! How did this happen? Did you fall?" I demanded.

"No! Willhelm Schwartz made me do it." He had stopped crying, but his eyes were still red.

"Made you do what?" I persisted.

"He was calling me names, so I hit him. Only he is bigger and stronger, so he hit me back," Peter explained with righteous indignation.

"You were fighting? You've never fought with anyone before. I thought Wilhelm was your friend. This is not like you, Peter!"

"But, Mama, he called me a bastard! I don't even know what it means. But all the other boys laughed and pointed at me, so I knew it was a bad word." Peter's tone quieted. "Am I a bastard, Mama?" His hazel eyes turned up toward me as I tenderly held his chin between my thumb and fingers.

So, there it was—the conversation I had been dreading. Father's eyes flared like a gas lantern igniting at nightfall. Until now, we had somehow managed to sidestep this issue. For the first four years of Peter's life, we could truthfully say his Papa was out of town working. Though Matthias's visits had been infrequent, Peter understood that this transient man somehow belonged to our family. Peter called my father Grosspapa or sometimes just Papa. He did not question Father's position as the head of the household. When Peter started school last year, he realized that the other fathers were much younger than his papa, but his childish mind did not judge such differences, just noted them.

The elder Herr Willhelm Schwartz had a long-standing grudge against Father. Many years ago, Father had intervened when Willhelm was rudely bullying his wife in public, humiliating and cursing her, causing consternation for all who witnessed his crude language and blatant disrespect. Out of spite, he referred to me as *rabenmutter* (raven mother)—a woman who "works"—with all its negative connotations and innuendos. He called my son the rabenmutter's bastard. The younger Willhelm was also a bully and as crass and vulgar as his father. He'd confronted my innocent Peter with a term Peter had never heard but which was clearly derogatory.

"Let's get you cleaned up. Your nose will heal. I don't think it's broken." I tried to divert his attention from the question looming over us.

"Mama, what's a bastard?" With downcast eyes, he pleaded for an explanation.

I searched Father's face, silently begging for rescue. He mutely turned his back and walked back to his room, leaving me behind to confront the enormous consequences of Matthias's rejection and abandonment and my own transgressions. Now, those consequences reverberated through my innocent son's life. I could not lie to Peter. It would only make things worse.

"Well, Peter, let me tell you a story. Once upon a time," I began, mimicking his favorite fairytales, "there was a young woman who loved a man. She loved him truly, and he loved her. But his love was not true. Their love for each other blended them together, like chocolate and milk blend to make the Swiss candies you get from St. Nicholas. Only their love did not make chocolate, it made you!"

Peter listened raptly as he did each evening when I read him his bedtime stories.

"As I said," I continued, "his love was not true, and he left the young fraulein alone to care for the beautiful chocolate they made together. That's you! But don't worry. This story has happy ending. The mother (that's me) was strong and smart. She gave her strength and cleverness to her little chocolate. Who's that?"

"That's me!" Peter smiled brightly as if he had just solved a riddle.

"You will be like the brave little tailor in Grimm's tale who outsmarts the giant." I grasped at any help I could find. The Brothers Grimm came to my rescue. It was easy to invoke the lessons of their stories. The Grimm brothers were from our Black Forest country, and their stories and fairy tales evoked the stories our mothers and grandmothers told us as children. Again, his face brightened.

"I love that story," he said. "The brave little tailor tricks the giant and the king every time he is put to the test. And I'm the little tailor, aren't I? Papa is a tailor, and you are a tailor, so doesn't that make me a tailor? If he calls me names again, I will find a way to trick him. He is not so smart, you know. He is strong and mean, but my marks in school are much better than his." Peter put on a brave face and set about plotting ways he could defend himself.

"You will be the smart one, the fast one, the boy with an agile mind who can solve problems. You will have a happy ending." I encouraged him.

But fairy tales could not defend my son. The teasing continued. His brave face hardened into a stern visage, protecting a vulnerable heart. Over time, he took comfort in piety and prayer, strictly adhering to the rules and commandments. If he could not overcome the sins of his mother, at least he could make sure no one could criticize his own commitment to morality. Peter hoped his good behavior would give him respectability. Abiding by the strictures of religion gave him a feeling of certainty.

By the time school ended in the spring, another rumor began flying through town. The pox had reappeared in a nearby town. I was determined that, this time, my family would not suffer the way Gilly had suffered, the way Francisca still suffered. I was desperate to protect my son.

When the old bookseller, Herr Frankel, next stopped by to tempt Father and me with his latest acquisitions, I blurted out my deepest fears. "Herr Frankel, have you heard of a pox outbreak in Freiburg?" He was a trusted friend and far more worldly than any of us. "Is it true?" I craved information from the wise, old man who did not share the superstitious beliefs of the townspeople about what caused the disease.

"Oh yes, a young girl in Freiburg contracted the pox. She did not die, but she was blinded by the disease," he reported without apparent sentiment. This was not comforting.

"I can't let this happen to Peter. I won't let this happen to Peter, even if I need to lock him up in the house." There was some reason to believe this would help, since the rich who sequestered themselves at their estates seemed to suffer less from the disease.

"I don't think that exposing him to red objects is a practical solution and neither is bloodletting, as many doctors practice. But I have heard there is a doctor in Strasburg who is using a new procedure called inoculation." Herr Frankel stroked his long beard thoughtfully.

"I think I read about this procedure in the *Freiburg Gazette*. It is very dangerous, isn't it? People have bad reactions to the inoculations, don't they? Aren't they actually injecting the disease into a healthy person?" I had a rudimentary familiarity with the idea of inoculation. It seemed like a primitive ritual, and I had not paid much attention to it. But now that the wolf was at the door, it seemed like an acceptable risk to keep him from entering.

"Yes, I suppose it is a bit dangerous, but it has gained wide acceptance in England. The doctor who perfected the technique, Dr. Jenner, is having excellent results. The instances of smallpox among his clients are far lower than in the rest of the population. Besides, he is not injecting smallpox into people; he is using a less harmful variety, cowpox. There are fewer bad effects, and it seems to make most of his patients immune to the disease." The good bookseller dragged a handkerchief across face. He suddenly seemed exhausted and very old.

"Please, Herr Frankel, sit down," Father chimed in. "My Anastasia is so caught up in her own concerns she has forgotten her manners. Now, what books do you have to show us today?" Herr Frankel sank gratefully into the upholstered chair in the corner of the shop. My mind raced as climbed the stairs to fetch a glass of cool water for the old book seller.

He had told me all I needed to hear. I was determined to find a doctor to give Peter the treatment. Father was against it. Mama was dubious but understood my urgent need to at least try to defend my son. Francisca, now twenty-five years old, was my greatest supporter. She, of all people, understood the devastation the pox could cause, even if you did not die from it. Together we started asking everyone who walked through our door if they knew a doctor who could visit our town and inoculate our children.

The townspeople were divided, as was our family. But many mothers, bent on doing whatever they could to protect their children, agreed that, if we could find a doctor who would come to us, they would pool their meager savings and pay his fee.

Francisca and I began a letter writing campaign. We wrote to all the guild halls within a two-day carriage ride, asking them to help us find a doctor who would travel to Gruntal.

For weeks, we heard nothing. Then one day a small, wizened man, carrying a black valise almost larger than he was arrived with the post carriage. After disembarking, he made his way to the market and immediately started asking, in an old-fashioned version of German tinged with a French accent, if anyone new a Franciscus Burkart. The little man presented such an odd appearance that people were immediately curious. It was quickly determined that he was looking for Francisca and was directed to the tailor's shop.

I greeted him in my usual respectful manner, turning my appraising eye to his wardrobe. He could certainly use a sartorial upgrade. His frock coat and breeches were black and terribly out of date. The fashion for men had shifted to trousers and loose blouses and away from these threadbare relics of the past. He wore a long, black coat that hung almost to his ankles. A tall, tube-shaped hat of fur sat on his head like a stovepipe.

"Is this where I might meet Franciscus Burkart?" His high, piping voice with its odd French-accented German resembled a shorebird calling at the water's edge.

"Guten Tag, Herr ..." I trailed off. "Might I know your name?"

"Yes, of course, I am Dr. Dreyfuss," he said, nodding to me in greeting. "My good friend, Herr Frankel the bookseller, mentioned your search for a doctor, and then I got this letter sent from the schneider's guild." There, in his hand, was the very letter we had sent to Strasburg. It was signed Franciscus Burkart, the male form of Francisca's name. No doubt she thought our request would have greater weight if it came from a man, rather than from a mere woman.

"Oh yes, of course. You are asking after my sister, Francisca. She and I wrote letters on behalf of the women of our town, seeking a doctor to inoculate our children against smallpox. Please make yourself comfortable. I will find Francisca." I directed him to the one upholstered chair in our shop. "Would you like tea? Or perhaps a beer?"

Without waiting for an answer, I left him sitting alone in our quiet shop and ran out the door in search of my sister, who had gone to market. By the time I returned, with Francisca in tow, both Father and Mama were sitting in the shop, chatting amiably with Herr Doctor Dreyfuss. Francisca forthrightly, and without a hint of shame, showed her scars to the doctor, who looked at them with professional curiosity.

As we conversed, Peter burst in the door, sending the little bell above the door into a noisy dance. He ran through the shop, head down, seemingly on an urgent mission. I caught him by the arm as he ran past me.

"This is my son, Peter." I introduced the squirming boy. "Say hello to Herr Doctor Dreyfuss," I instructed. "He is here to save you from the pox."

"But I don't have the pox. I don't need saving." Peter's alarm was written on his face.

"Most, well, some of the women of the town have banded together to protect our children from the most recent outbreak of pox," I explained, ready to launch into a detailed explanation of our campaign to recruit supporters and a doctor to administer the inoculations.

Herr Doctor Dreyfuss rose abruptly and ended the conversation, apparently not feeling that young boys needed lengthy explanations. "Well, let's start at once. I will meet anyone who would like my services. I will start tomorrow morning, here in this place." His manner was like that of a field marshal, terse and authoritative. He did not hesitate to commandeer our shop as his clinic.

"Peter, you go to the homes of all your classmates and tell their mothers that Dr. Dreyfuss will inoculate their children here, tomorrow morning."

Peter objected, but a stern warning glance from Dr. Dreyfuss set him on the right path, and off he ran, on a new, more important mission.

The next morning dawned cool and overcast. Mist shrouded the river and a thin, light drizzle deposited one sparkling, dewy drop at the tip of each blade of grass. I arose at daybreak to open the shop. Early though it was, dozens of mothers and squirming children crowded the street in front of our shop. I pushed the bolts of fabric on a back shelf into a corner; scooped up the detritus of yesterday's unfinished work; and unceremoniously deposited the thread, needles, and scraps of fabric in a heap.

As soon as I opened the door, men, women and children poured in from the street. The crowd included determined mothers, hecklers, naysayers, and even a few who threw tomatoes at the door. Francisca calmly organized the people into an orderly queue that snaked out the door and down the street.

"He's a Jew!" a heavyset man in the back growled. "He will try to kill them. Don't you know Jews poison the wells and place curses on our crops to make them fail? He will kill your children."

A low growl of disapproval rumbled through the crowd like an angry dog.

A shudder passed from one soul to the next. Feet shuffled, and people muttered unintelligibly. Some withdrew from the line and stood to the side, undecided.

"He is a doctor! He knows more than you do! I will laugh when your children are chewed up by the pox and mine grow up healthy, with flawless skin." One brave mother raised her voice to answer the crows of doom. "Do you remember the last time smallpox swept through? Francisca certainly does," she crowed again, pointing frankly at my sister.

Francisca, who spent most of her life shrinking from the gaze of others, bravely stepped forth. She faced directly into the crowd and pulled her shift down around her shoulders. Her skin was stippled with pits that spread across her face and shoulders. A collective gasp arose. Where others saw disfiguring scars, I saw only beauty and bravery.

Undaunted, many brave mothers surged into line, queuing their sons and daughters up to undergo the fearful, unfamiliar, possibly painful procedure. One by one, the children submitted to sharply pronged tines that poked into their arms like a fork-tongued snake, carrying the venom of cowpox into their bodies. The children squirmed and flinched, but the presence of their peers made them behave much more bravely than they otherwise might have done. The only ones who cried were the young children and, very often, their mothers. We could only hope and pray that we were not subjecting our children to this invasion of their bodies in vain.

Dr. Dreyfuss ignored the jeers as he calmly made his way past the waiting crowd and took up his position at the table in the shop. He opened his black bag with practiced efficiency and methodically laid out his tools.

The inoculations continued throughout the day. The terse, efficient Dr. Dreyfuss steeped the tines in alcohol between each child. By the end of the day, it was over. A few last stragglers hurried in, pushing open the door as we began closing the shop.

"We've ridden all day, down from the mountain! Are we too late? We just heard there was a doctor saving children from smallpox here today. My brother died in the last pox outbreak. I have a son. I simply cannot lose another loved one." She breathlessly sought to explain her late arrival. She was about my age, standing right in front of me, telling her story that was also my story. It was like looking into a mirror. Her son stepped up, bared his arm and wordlessly received the doctor's last dose.

About a week later, Peter developed a fever and then a rash. I suffered panic, thinking I would be the cause of his death. I prayed more fervently than I had ever done. Within a week, the rash disappeared. The fever abated. The crisis had passed. Peter would not succumb to the ravages of a disease that had killed and scarred thousands of people. Mothers and fathers congregated on every street corner comparing the reactions endured by their offspring. Some were severe and some quite mild, but no one died, developed scars, or any other permanent reminder of their ordeal, other than a small, stippled scar on his or her arm.

After ravaging nearby towns and villages, the pox marched from the Rhine up the hills through our beautiful little valley and into the mountains beyond. It appeared first among the farming villages and then in the towns. The familiar tragedy played itself out as it had in similar outbreaks for hundreds of years. Nearly half the children died and many more suffered devastating long-term consequences, but our children were spared.

As it had been after Napoleon's war, when I distributed simple aprons to the mothers of our dead boys, I received thanks and respect from many of the townspeople. But I was not the brave one. I was merely terrified and desperate. It was the other brave mothers who, in concert, had pulled the plow of progress, dragging our town out of superstition and into a new century of medical progress.

* * *

A steady rhythm ran through my days, from throwing the shutters open in the morning to working by lamplight in the evening. I remained the same, but around me things were changing. Father's health deteriorated markedly. He seemed to have shrunk. His strong shoulders stooped. His breathing became labored. He made fewer and fewer appearances in the tailor shop. Still, he attended the guild meetings as often as he could, taking pride in his long career as the town's tailor. He continued to contribute to the community in any way he could. But even his supporters could no longer hold back the surge of young craftsmen unable to find guild-sponsored work.

In many towns, these young men, coming back from their stints as journeymen with skills and youthful vigor, began to practice their occupations without the blessing of the guilds. They set up small shops on the outskirts of town or in some out-of-the-way neighborhood outside the range of guild supervision. Rather than risk erosion of their professional standards and control, the guild elders decided that we must accept at least one new master schneider.

And so it was, on an evening not unlike that summer evening so many years ago, when I first made my case for becoming Father's apprentice, the guild masters announced to Father that they would authorize a new master tailor in our town. This time, there was no argument or stalling tactic that would postpone the inevitable. Father walked home to break the news to me. I watched him approach, knowing what the outcome would be and knowing there was nothing we could do to prevent it. I would never become a master schneider. Father's frame, bent with age and frailty, demonstrated the necessity of the decision.

"Father, can I get you some kuchen or a nice stein of beer?" I greeted my poor Father as a loving daughter.

He looked up at me, standing next to his chair. "My dear Anastasia, you know there was nothing I could do, don't you?"

The understanding between us was profound. We knew each other so well. We had worked together so long; he did not even need to explain. How was it that, caught up in the day-to-day bustle of running a business, we'd never planned for this day? Now I knew my innocent, girlish wish to become an independent woman had come true. Father was fading. I would be the sole support of my family. But this was not the glorious victory I had imagined it would be.

"You need not explain, Father. I understand." I rested my hand on his shoulder both to comfort him and to physically feel the closeness between us. Without turning to look at me, he placed his hand, with its protruding network of blue veins and its fingertips, calloused from years of pushing the needle, on top of mine. He patted my hand gently.

"What will this mean to us? To our family?" This time it was Father asking me the unanswerable questions, hoping I would come up with an ingenious solution.

But I would never be a master schneider. There was little I could do. "We will be fine, Father. We will continue to work. Our customers will continue to come to us, despite the new schneider. After all, haven't we served them faithfully all these years? We will find our way." I was now the adult comforting the child. It was an uncomfortable role reversal. And I wasn't nearly as confident as my brave words implied.

The new tailor set up his shop as far from ours as he could and still be well situated. Gruntal was not tiny, but neither was it large. An hour's time was sufficient to walk from one end to the other, so it was inevitable that our customers, no matter how loyal, would at least pay the new schneider a call, if only to satisfy their curiosity. The new schneider's shop was very appealing. At least that's what Peter told me, after he paid the new shop a visit to satisfy his own curiosity.

"It is new! It's nice. Everything is clean and orderly. The fabrics are colorful and don't have layers of dust dulling them." He enthused. "He should be tending trees," Peter smiled at his joke. "That's what his name, Baumgartner, means—tree gardener." Maybe he was trying to defend us in his childish way, by joking at our rival's expense. But he went on. "He is young, maybe younger than you, Mama. And he is cheerful. I think the ladies really like him."

Really? I thought. The ladies? I had never considered that the appeal of a handsome young man might be my greatest competition. By opening his shop on the outer edge of town, Herr Baumgartner was able to attract the farmers who would consider a walk or cart ride into town too big an effort but who could easily walk to the outskirts. Using the services of a guild tailor was a luxury. Their wives, whether good seamstresses or not, had always sewn the family's garments. It was a mark of success and prestige to be able to have a real tailor provide them one nicely fitted jacket they could proudly wear to Sunday Mass.

Not only that, but by being closer to the edge of town, he could more easily trade with the rural fabric weavers. Father and I had always traded in the best markets for the finest handcrafted fabrics we would find, or from wide-ranging Jewish merchants who brought the best fabrics with the most attractive prints and patterns to us from distant places, and from fabric merchants in nearby larger town markets. We never bought directly from the peasants, as the quality of their fabrics varied widely.

Lately, however, factories with mechanical looms powered by steam engines, like those in the north, at Aachen and Krefeld, were changing the age-old craft of weaving. Weavers, never highly paid to begin with, were being drawn to the factories where fabrics were manufactured in quantities not achievable by individuals. The less prosperous weavers, particularly the young and the women, could earn a steady income in these factories. The fabrics they manufactured were far less expensive, and this produced pressure on the home weavers to cut their prices. Herr Baumgartner negotiated very good prices from area weavers, so the prices of his garments were very affordable.

My days became less busy. The bell over the door rang less frequently. I busied myself cleaning and reorganizing the shop to show off our wares to their best advantage. I repainted our sign. I even hired a stonemason to embed a mosaic of a scissors made of small, smoothly polished river stones into the cobblestone at the front of our shop, as I had seen craftsmen of Freiburg do.

Finally, I succumbed to curiosity and defensiveness. I donned my best Sunday dress and jacket, a small, finely-made hat and marched across town to Herr Baumgartner's new shop.

Peter was right. The shop was small but tidy and colorful. The bolts of fabric were arrayed on cleverly designed shelves that marched up the walls like the shelves in a fine library. But these shelves could be pulled out from the wall on runners, making it easy to see each bolt individually.

"Guten Tag, Fraulein Burkart," Herr Baumgartner said when I entered as he pushed one of his clever shelves back into its place against the wall. He flashed a charming smile at me. I was disarmed at once. How did he know who I was?

"Guten Tag, Herr Baumgartner." I did not smile. I squared my shoulders, stood as tall as I could, and held my chin high. I could not look him straight in the eye as I had intended.

"I …I …" I fumbled for words. What had I come here to say? My well-planned dissertation on upholding the standards of the craft fled from my mind. "Where did you get these shelves?" I blurted out. "I've never seen anything like it."

"My father was a fine wood craftsman and an inventor." I had not expected such candor about his personal background. "He invented this system." As if we had known each other for years, he beckoned me close and pulled out a drawer to show me the device.

"Small, well-oiled marbles line narrow troughs in runners that support the shelves. They allow the shelf to slide on top of the marbles." He lifted his head from his shelves and showed me his charming smile again.

"Remarkable," was all I could say. I stood awkwardly, shifting my weight from one foot to another as we stood in the middle of his shop, unspeaking. Finally, I got a grip on my resolve and inelegantly challenged him. "I came here to see for myself what Herr Burkart and I are up against." I thrust my chin out more than I had intended.

"Really?" He showed no sign of defensiveness. A hint of a smile tugged at his tightly pursed lips. "And have you decided that I am your opponent?"

"Well, yes. Of course!" I paused, suddenly less sure of myself. "Aren't you? Father and I have never had to compete for customers before." I was the one who sounded defensive.

He smiled at me indulgently as you would at a wayward child. "You see I have set my shop up as far from yours as I could. You see I have brought into my shop customers who were not your customers, who were never before anyone's customers. I do not have a dress form in my shop, because I do not intend to become a designer of women's fashions. I respect your father very much. No one at the guild has one bad word to say about him." He paused.

Again, I could not find words.

"Nor against you, I might add." He bowed slightly in my direction.

Now I was completely off guard.

"By the way, how is Herr Burkart? I hope he is in good health." He sounded genuinely concerned, completely sincere.

"Father is well," I started. I simply could not keep up my pretense of combativeness. "Actually you see, Herr Baumgartner, he is getting older. I have most of the responsibility for the business." I raised my eyes to his. They were gray-green, not unlike my own. His curly, dark hair caught the afternoon light, showing roan highlights.

"As I understand it, this is not a new situation for you. You have been working at his side for many years already. Is this not true?" His voice was neutral, neither condemning my position as a working woman nor treating it like anything special. How had he come to know so much about me? I wondered at the efficiency of the spiderweb-like threads of communication in our small town.

"Yes," I said, straightening to my full height. "I am perfectly capable of sustaining our business by my efforts alone." Though my voice was strong, my heart was fluttering.

"Well then, Fraulein Burkart, you have nothing to fear from me. I'm sure you have seen how the town is growing. The production of fabric, as you might be aware, is changing. I expect that, soon enough, there will be more changes. We must keep abreast of the times in which we live. I will do nothing to hurt you that time itself would not accomplish without me."

Did he intend to comfort me? I found his statements both frank and disquieting. Again, for a moment, I was at a loss for words. Finally, I found my tongue. "Yes, well, I'm sure you are correct. Thank you for your time. I trust we will see each other as we go about our separate businesses." I tried to sound as gracious as he. I had no idea if I had succeeded. "Guten Tag, Herr Baumgartner."

I turned and left the shop without risking any further embarrassment. I could not resist a final look over my shoulder at this handsome young man standing in his doorway, a whimsical smile upon his lips.

* * *

By 1833, it was clear that our clientele was declining. Apart from my dressmaking clients, those loyal souls who still came to our shop were as old as father. As often as not, they came to converse with Father as much as to tend to their garments. I still had women customers who liked working with a woman who had both tailoring skill and a woman's sense of style. I enjoyed dressmaking and was grateful for the camaraderie of other women. We talked and laughed and exchanged gossip. Father's respectable male customers looked askance at us, casting sidelong glances at the chatty women in the shop.

Francisca did her best to contribute to the family economy. She doubled her efforts in the garden, even taking some of her surplus to the weekly market in the harvest season. This was deeply humiliating for me and Father, but neither of us had the heart to say anything to Francisca. She was trying to help. She had very little social life, and the market stall was a chance for her to exchange pleasantries with our neighbors and the other vendors. Mama carried on with household chores as best she could. Though she was seven years younger than Father, she was well past sixty years old, and she too was also slowing down.

"Who wants to attend a hen party?" Father reprimanded me one evening after a rare full day in the shop with me. "I saw Herr Dunkel come to the door, and actually turn and leave when he heard you and your friends cackling."

"I had no idea!" I replied. My heart sank. Was this really the reason our business was falling off? I didn't know what to do to attract more male customers, now that they had an alternative at Herr Baumgartner's shop. All I could do was try to maintain a more professional decorum in the shop. I stopped serving kaffee to my women customers. That discouraged the women from overstaying the time it took to tend to business and from congregating at the shop when they did not have any dressmaking needs. I tried to pay more attention to the needs of the men customers.

Another winter came and went. Another spring resurrected hopefulness, as spring always does. The summer of 1831 arrived as peacefully as puffy clouds drifting in the blue sky. One morning in early summer, Mother rose early to tend the cooking stove, boil water for tea, and crack eggs for breakfast. She was tired as she dragged through her morning routine. Peter, age eight, came into the kitchen early. He could not break his fast before receiving Holy Communion, so he sat at the table with only a cup of water. The Church dictated that the body of Christ must be the first thing you ate if you wanted to take communion. For Peter, this meant he often started the day without breakfast. Though he was born without the benefit of legitimacy, he had badgered Father Schmidt into allowing him to become an altar boy. He studied diligently, memorizing the sequence of bell ringing, genuflecting, responding at the right times with the right Latin phrases, and moving about the altar in the timeless ritual of the Mass.

"Go up and check on your grosspapa," Mama said without looking up from her eggs.

"But I'll be late!" Peter protested. The last thing Peter wanted was to make the slightest misstep, lest the privilege of serving the Mass be taken away from him. He ran down the stairs and out the door before he could be restrained.

"Francisca, would you please go and wake your father? He will be late for his breakfast." Mama asked.

Francisca, always demurely cooperative, stood up from snapping the tips off her green beans, put her bowl down on the kitchen table, and gently knocked on Father's door. When he did not respond, she carefully pushed the door open. He lay in his bed peacefully, his head canted at an awkward angle.

She gingerly shook his shoulder. Then she shook a little harder. She bent to look into his face. It was grayish white. Instinctively, she touched his face. Cold.

"Mama! Anastasia!" She was choking and coughing.

Without another word, Mama and I ran to the bedroom door. I already knew what to expect. I lingered at the door to the bedroom Father had shared with Mama for so long, hesitant to go in. Mama rushed past me to the bedside.

"He's cold. He's so cold. How could I not have noticed? I've slept in the same bed with him for thirty-six years, and I did not even notice when he died at my side!" Mama was horrified by this guilty realization. She wailed helplessly.

I entered the room silently, barely breathing. I knelt next to him and took his cold hand in mine. "Father, I'm here. If your spirit is still in this room, please know how much I have loved you. Please know how terribly I will miss you. Please go in peace, knowing I am here to take care of our family." I rested my forehead against his still chest. I felt the gorge rising, my throat clenching, my eyes burning. My tears began to fall. I tried to absorb the last ounces of strength from my father's spirit. Mama's wails and Francisca's moans bounced off the walls around me as I collapsed silently to the floor.

CHAPTER 9

A HOUSEHOLD OF WOMEN

1835–1836

Winter had been brutally cold, cold enough to paint the inside of the windowpanes with ice as thick as felted wool. Water froze in the washbasins. By February 1835, the days were noticeably longer, but the temperatures stayed stubbornly below freezing. Mama had been fading, winding down like an old clock. We made Peter sleep with Mama, while Francisca and I shared a bed, just to keep each other warm in our cocoons of heavy winter blankets. Peter, now twelve years old, was deeply offended by being forced to sleep with his oma.

Oma was a noisy sleeper; her snoring had only gotten worse with age. Her mental capacities had declined rapidly since Father's death. She could not keep a thought in her head for the time it took to walk from the kitchen to the pantry. She often drifted off in midsentence or addressed me as if I was her sister, talking about events from her girlhood as if they'd happened yesterday. Like a child's neatly stacked blocks swept into disarray by a little sister, the events of her life, instead of progressing in orderly sequence from the earliest to the most recent, lay in hopeless jumble.

One morning, as she had done every morning for decades, she rose from the bed to rekindle the cooking fire in the old stove to put the morning pot of water on to boil. But this morning was different. Instead of warm steam and the aroma of strong kaffee greeting our nostrils, we were met with a noxious smell.

"What's going on, Mama?" I chided, trying to sound calm.

She looked at me with a vacant expression and resumed stirring the pot as though she hadn't heard me. I looked into the vessel and realized Mama had picked up the chamber pot from the foot of her bed and placed it on the stove.

"Good grief! Did Mama have an accident in the kitchen?" Francisca coughed and gagged.

"Look at what's in the pot!" I exclaimed.

Peter found the incident hilarious in the way only a twelve-year-old boy could. "Wait until I tell the boys." He was sure to have the best story of the week, maybe the month, among the altar boys who were his closest friends.

"Don't you dare!" I exploded. "You will not belittle your oma in her frailty. And you will not dishonor this family."

Peter turned sour, mumbling something about me not being the one to talk about dishonoring the family. I let the derogatory remark pass without comment.

"Here," I said, thrusting the chamber pot into his hands. "Take this outside and dump it in the outhouse. And you'll not mention the incident again."

With a sinking sensation in the pit of my stomach, I realized that the simplistic explanation of his birth I'd given to Peter as a young boy was not going to be adequate for Peter as a youth.

By the time the ice started to melt in March, Mama had begun coughing. She grew very weak, losing weight rapidly. Though Francisca and I did not know the cause of her coughing, we immediately decided to give her exclusive use of one of our two bedrooms. Only Francisca was allowed to enter to check on her. That seemed to soothe Mama. Peter moved from his comfortable but noisy bed with Mama to a pallet in the pantry.

"I'll be the one to deal with Mama. I have survived a serious illness that killed others. If our experience with inoculations taught us something, perhaps it was that surviving illnesses gives us resistance to them. I have not had this coughing disease, but I will trust God and my strong constitution to give me resistance to this one also. Besides, I am closer to Mama. She and I have spent our lives making a home for our family, while you worked alongside Father in the shop." Thirty-year-old Francisca now had the confidence of a grown woman. And she spoke the truth, as much as it stung to admit it.

Her reasoning was so clear and her heart so true that there was no point in arguing with her. Francisca brought Mama her meals and read to her from Peter's book of folktales by the Brothers Grimm. Mama enjoyed being read to, and these folktales reminded her of the stories told by her own mother and grandmother. It was sometimes difficult to tell if she was asleep or awake. She lay flat on her back motionless, her head turned to the wall. At times, we could not tell if she was breathing, until a violent, wracking fit of coughing overtook her, leaving her even weaker than before. Soon, Mama was so weak she could no longer get out of bed. Francisca dealt with the difficulties—the sleeplessness, the mess of her bedpan, the broth dribbling down her cheek when she tried to feed her—with uncomplaining grace.

One morning, Francisca came out of Mama's room with a dour look. "She is coughing blood now. I must change her bedclothes every day, or she may drown in her own sweat. Should we call a doctor?" Her expression was grim, her eyes sunk into their sockets. Though she never complained, she was growing weary.

"Let's wait a day or two. Sometimes the sick need to sweat out their illness to purge it. Maybe the sweating is a sign that she is recovering. The doctor has one treatment for everything, regardless of the symptoms. He slashes an arm and lets the blood flow out. Mama is so weak, I can't believe that his barbaric treatment would do her any good." I tried to justify my position. In my heart, I was afraid of what the doctor would say. There was no hope.

Two days later, Mama died. We wrapped her in her bedclothes and carried her down to the shop. She weighed almost nothing. My handsome, strong, square-jawed Mama with the sad, gray eyes and quiet voice was gone.

There is a feeling that comes over you when both of your parents are gone. Even though I was thirty-nine years old, I felt as though I had just become a fully adult woman for the first time. Even though I had shouldered great responsibility for our family for years, while my parents were alive, I felt like a child. That child within me longed to cling to the mother who, despite her own troubles, had struggled to raise me as best she could. Even though I was no older than I had been the day before, I suddenly felt I was a part of the older generation, those old *faltige alte frauen* (wrinkled old women) who lurked around the edges of festivals, weddings, and dances.

Francisca and I clung to each other. Two women and one young son who was quickly growing up and drifting away were the remnants of our once lively, young family.

Though he was pious, serious, and applied himself to his studies as best he could, Peter did not stand out as one of the brightest boys. I fretted and worried over what the future would bring for my Peter. I could not bring him into the business as my father had done for me. The business had dwindled markedly after Father's death. I did not have status in the guild, so I could not sponsor my son. The men who had been Father's longstanding customers no longer had a sense of personal loyalty and soon drifted to Herr Baumgartner. My women customers still came to me, but their patronage alone was not enough to sustain all of us. I could not ask Herr Baumgartner to take Peter as an apprentice because he lacked one of the guild's crucial requirements to be his or anyone else's apprentice—legitimacy.

As the snow of the winter melted after Mama's death, Peter himself solved the problem of his future. The Schultz family still ran one of the most prosperous farms in the area. Their Riesling grapes were of the highest quality. They also grew our valley's famous early plums, a large variety of vegetables for the market, and hops for beer making. They raised pigs, chickens, and a few dairy cows. After Napoleon's war, Rupert's younger brother, Clem, worked with the senior Herr Schultz and took over the operations of the farm when his father passed away. Clem, Gilly's old playmate, was now thirty-five years old, a grown man with a small family of young children. His sisters had married and moved away from the home place. He was forced to resort to hired men for his farm labor. His laborers were often young men adrift, always waiting for a chance to make their own way in the world. While most of them were reliable, they did not last long on the Schultz farm. They came and went. A new cast of characters appeared each spring.

In 1836, when Peter turned thirteen, he developed the habit of disappearing each afternoon. He was always home in time for supper and showed little inclination to make trouble as did many boys his age, so I never questioned him about where he was or what he was doing. In early winter, when the world was brown and dead but before the snow started to cover the ground, Peter came home at supper time with Clem Schultz in tow.

"My goodness, Clem, what a surprise! I certainly wasn't expecting a visit from you. Please come in. We don't have much, but Francisca is a wonderful cook. We have potato soup, apple strudel, and kaffee. Please, sit down," I said, perplexed but genuinely happy to see him.

I busied myself with setting the table for our guest and warmed the kaffee. I bustled around, as much to cover my confusion as to be hospitable.

We sat across the table from each other. Clem had his brother Rupert's same cleft chin, blue eyes, and wavy hair. My mind drifted back to the years when I was young and hopeful and sure the world would be generous to me.

"Ahem," Clem coughed, studying his kaffee intently.

"Oh, I'm so sorry. I was daydreaming. I apologize. I'm sure you came here with a purpose. Please feel free to speak." I tried to dispel his discomfort and let him come right to the point.

"Well, Fraulein Burkart, actually I came to ask if you could help me." He looked up; his discomfort suddenly evaporated.

"Really? Well, of course I can help you! Are you looking for trousers? Or perhaps a new winter coat?" I hoped my eagerness for the work was not too transparent.

"No, no. It's not that. I would like to ask you if you could spare Peter."

"Peter?" I could sense my eyes widen and my eyebrows lift in surprise.

"Yes, my children are too young to be of much help. Peter has been helping me each afternoon without my asking. He has been very useful and resourceful. There is no task he will not bend his back to. I would like him to be my helper in the fields, so I can devote more effort to the office work for which I never seem to have time. He can take his meals with us. I will find a warm place for his pallet. I will treat him as one of our family." He finally took a breath

It was as if he was throwing buckets of water at my face. I could only sputter and shake my head. "My goodness! This is a surprise! Peter is only thirteen years old. He should stay in school for a few more years." I tried to think of what Father would have said.

"Peter, what do you think of this arrangement?" I turned to see his hazel eyes sparkling with delight. His serious expression softened into something that resembled longing.

"I know I can do this work. Tante Mausi—I mean Aunt Francisca—has taught me to love the soil and understand the needs of growing plants. I am strong and healthy. I will learn so much from Herr Schultz. Aunt Francisca did not attend school, and she learned everything she needs to know." I had not seen him this ardent since he struggled to learn the arcane rituals of the Mass as an altar boy.

I turned back to Clem. "Will you be able to pay him?"

My directness surprised him. But he did not hesitate or apologize, only answered with equal directness. "No, at least not at first. He will receive room and board and tutoring in every aspect of farming, viticulture, dairy farming, and orchard keeping, as well as animal husbandry. We will see what the future will bring. We can talk about pay in a couple of years, after he no longer needs much instruction. Our farm, as you know, is not a simple peasant farm. In the beginning, I will need to spend much time instructing him. But later …" He trailed off.

He explained so quickly and convincingly that a pallet in the children's room was beginning to sound like a featherbed with clean linen sheets. He made it seem like a splendid opportunity, as if Peter would be attending the university of farming.

"Can I have a day or two to think this over?" I demurred from jumping at the opportunity to have Peter happily situated in this promising, if humble, position.

Herr Schultz rose from the table, leaving his kaffee and soup untouched and promising to pay me another visit in three days.

Peter immediately devoured the abandoned strudel. Peter was getting much bigger. He resembled his father, Matthias Kist, in so many ways— his straight-spined build, his tall frame, his serious demeanor. I looked at him with new eyes. As hard as I tried, we were never truly close. I felt I must be both father and mother to the boy. His resemblance to his father sometimes caused a pang of guilt and shame. My feelings were not Peter's fault. Although we loved each other, we had always held each other at arm's length. He had no such reserve with Francisca. He had often helped her in the garden. I could sometimes hear them laughing and singing as the shadows lengthened among the berry bushes. Together, they had turned every inch of space behind our house into a productive oasis of beauty and utility.

As it had been with me when I'd suggested to Father that I could be his apprentice, the answer was a foregone conclusion. If that's what he wanted, of course I would let Peter go to the Schultz's household. Now we would truly be a household of women.

The world was changing. At times I could almost smell the change in their air. I still loved to take the occasional ramble in the hills surrounded by the comforting sights and smells of the dark forests. Looking down at our town from the hills above, I could see the changes. I saw fewer and fewer fallow fields, as farmers planted as much land as they could. Many more roads curved out to the west toward the Rhine. The roads brought more commerce. People from towns once considered far away now crowded our local market with goods formerly considered exotic. I was even able to buy the *Freiburg Gazette* and no longer had to rely on the good graces of Herr Frankel for news of the world outside our town.

A few years ago, in 1832, an enormous gathering of more than twenty thousand men, women, workers, and students had held a "festival" at the castle at Neustadt. They'd marched from the market up the hill to the old, ruined castle. There, they made eloquent speeches pressing for unity among the thirty-nine German states. Each state had its own laws for currencies, weights, measures, and customs. The plethora of duties and taxes between states hampered trade and created isolation between each small province. The festival speakers spoke ardently of how strong we could be if we could unite together into one great country. Many of Napoleon's reforms had been rolled back when the margraves had reestablished their power after Napoleon's war. But the powerful ideas of Napoleon's time had not died with him. Young firebrands spoke of establishing political freedom, national unity, and equality for all people, even the women. The brave words of this Hambach Festival, as it came to be called, drifted away on the wind. But the winds of change continued to blow, and I could feel them gathering strength.

Now those winds blew through our echoing rooms as well. We were two unmarried women, no longer young—Francisca age thirty-one and myself age forty. The house felt strangely hollow. We were by ourselves but not alone. Although Peter no longer clomped heavily up the stairs, dead babies, a lost brother, and the ever-present ghosts of Mama and Father still inhabited this place with us. We could feel their presence. Sometimes I woke up in the morning, eager to rush down to the shop to tell Father about my latest idea for a dress design before the reality that he was gone made my heart sink. Each time it felt as if he had died again. Some mornings I could hardly get out of bed. Yet I dragged myself downstairs, threw open the shutters, and waited for the bell over the door to signal the arrival of the day's business. The bell, however, rang less and less frequently.

In the lamp-lit evenings, while Francisca read, darned stockings, or tatted, I hunched over the ledgers, my quill scratching loudly against the wall of our silence. Our income was dangerously low. I knew I would need to change with the changing times. I was responsible for my sister and myself. My dream of being an independent woman had been truly realized, but not as I had imagined it. I could hear my own voice telling Father, "I am strong and smart. You told me so yourself." In my dreams, Father whispered in my ear. "Remember who you are. You are my daughter. You are my Anastasia."

CHAPTER 10

INTO THE WOODS

1838

Francisca and I laughed together as we hefted huge baskets of vegetables for the market. It was midsummer, and we rose as soon as the dawn turned the eastern sky a rosy peach. Every Wednesday, local merchants set up their tables and stalls in the square surrounding the church.

"I want to be the first to set up my display in the market," Francisca enthused. "I have the most beautiful produce. Don't you agree? I will be the envy of all. I have a good clientele now, you know. People seek out my stand." Francisca, now thirty-three years old, had grown into her womanhood with grace and a certain pent-up energy, stored away during her lonely childhood.

She had outgrown her self-consciousness about being seen in public and had gathered a few loyal friends.

"You know, when you were a child, I thought you were a big baby, clinging to Mama all the time. Now look at you—the empress of the garden!" I was proud of my younger sister.

"And I thought you were a self-important snob, always huddling with Father about this and that." Her straight, white teeth gleamed as she smiled happily. Her sweet nature seemed to erase her physical scars. "We are in the same boat now, aren't we? Now, I am your partner." She seemed to glow from within, proud to be earning money. Her earnings were becoming more important to us.

As the sun peaked over the tops of the buildings, the market came to life. Tables and makeshift tents popped up in all corners of the square. Eventually they sorted themselves into more or less orderly rows according to the goods being sold. Huge rounds of cheese, pastries, bread, jams, and jellies gave way to aromatic bundles of herbs and spices. Everything from flowers to metal chains, harnesses to leather straps, and fresh eggs to dead chickens was on display, each item adding to the stew of smells on market day. Francisca settled into her stall, behind her impressive display of fresh vegetables. I helped as much as I could and then tore myself away, walking slowly and inhaling deeply as I returned to the tailor shop.

Once there, I puttered about, rearranging the tools I would need for the day, placing the dress form with my latest creation outside the front door, where no passerby could miss it. It displayed a simple, practical dress, modest but not too plain. The bodice fabric was a finely pin-striped maroon linen fashioned to cross over in front, mimicking the look of a peasant's shoulder scarf. The voluminous skirt was gathered at the waist to emphasize the slim waistline set off by a simple maroon silk ribbon. The sleeves hugged the arms from shoulder to hands and a border of lace peaked out from beneath at the wrists. I intended this to attract enough customers to feed us for the next month or two. Today I hoped the people from the countryside, drawn to town for market day, might make the little bell over the door sing.

Each week, Clem and his young wife, Hilda, generously invited us to share Sunday dinner with their family. It was a welcome respite. I would not say Francisca and I were lonely; we had neighbors and customers to talk to nearly every day. But amid the energy and activity of the Schultz family's three youngsters, all under seven, our everyday worries completely dropped away.

And it was a lovely excuse to see Peter. How he had grown! At sixteen he was truly a young man, big and muscular, with a deep voice. Only his boyishly handsome face gave away his youth.

After dinner, Clem leaned back in his chair, lit his pipe, and dove right into the conversation. "Well, Anastasia, how is your business going?" Clem, ever the direct, straightforward man, didn't bother with formality.

"I don't know, Clem. One day it seems all is well. Three good prospects for dresses will walk in the door. Then sometimes, for weeks on end, piecework and simple alterations are the only work I have."

"Have you ever thought of offering to pick up seamstress work at people's homes and deliver it when you've finished it?" Hilda was trying to be helpful, but to me this idea seemed somehow demeaning, more like the work of a peddler than that of a craftsman.

I shook my head. "No, I haven't considered that. Father never had to do anything of the sort. The work always came to him."

"Yes, but that was long ago." Hilda was young, and things that were very recent to me seemed like ages ago to her young mind.

"There are so many new people in town. They did not know your father, and they don't know you. The town has grown so much. People feel free to offer whatever services they can, regardless of whether they have the guild's permission or not." Young though she was, she was observant, her vision less clouded by what used to be or what might have been.

"Yes, that's true. The days of orderly, well-regulated crafts and trades seem to be disappearing." I agreed. Hilda was right of course.

The guilds were quickly losing the tight grip they'd had on commerce for centuries. Prussia, our huge neighbor to the north, had enlisted many of the smaller nearby states to join an important new trade arrangement. Together, they'd agreed to trade with each other using standard weights, measures, and currency. But most importantly, they traded without tariffs. Though the margrave of the State of Baden jealously held on to his sovereignty, this so-called Zollverein upset the balance. Those wishing to establish themselves as tradesmen felt empowered to take their skills anywhere that seemed promising, hang up their shingle, and attempt to establish themselves. Our population was growing rapidly, but so was competition for customers.

"You know, Anastasia, it's not a bad idea," Clem chimed in. "I seem to remember a time when you came to our home with an embroidered apron for my Mama. I was very young, but I remember it because the apron made her cry."

But it seemed wrong to me to equate my mission of compassion with a complete change in how I offered my services. I smiled. "That was different. Everyone was suffering so much. I just wanted to do something to make people happy. I was much younger then, too." My arguments sounded weak and irrelevant, even as I made them.

"I don't remember those times. I was too young," said Hilda. "But if you visited people's homes to give them your work then, why couldn't you do that now?"

I had to admit Hilda's simple, uncomplicated logic made sense. "Well, I'll give it some thought."

And I did think. Other than my pride, I could not see anything that would prevent me from seeking out customers rather than waiting for them to come to me.

The seed was planted. For weeks after, I thought of ways I could make this idea work.

Though it seemed somehow a betrayal of Father's business, it piqued my interest to plan how much to charge, how to introduce my service, and how to discover new customers. I worked at the ledgers in the evenings, figuring just how much income I would need to provide an adequate living for my sister and me. I planned efficient routes that wound around town streets, country lanes, and even up into my cherished hills and dark forests. A little damaged pride seemed a small price to pay to make a better living, so I immersed myself in my new project.

I began by visiting all the homes I had visited after Napoleon's war. Then I knocked on the doors of strangers. No one treated me rudely; I told myself there was no reason to be afraid, no reason to be humiliated.

The work I generated walking my routes was easy—simple alternations and repairs, a new apron, a child's smock. But my skills were well appreciated, especially by the far flung wives who seldom made the trip to town. I sometimes bartered my work for more expensive items, like a good shoulder of beef for pot roast, or new shoes. But there were limitations I had not anticipated. I spent most of my daylight hours walking the neighborhoods, climbing trails to outlying farms and hamlets. My evenings were spent doing close needlework by lamplight. The tailor shop went unattended for many hours each day.

In the honey-colored light of one September afternoon, I walked the trails above the town feeling stronger than I had in years. I was on my way to deliver some mended sheets, darned stockings, and a few undergarments to a customer on the western reaches of town. The air at this precarious time of year smelled fecund, hovering between ripeness and decay. It was a cloudless late autumn day. The shady mountain tracks crackled with autumn leaves, and the dark firs bent to whisper their names in the light breeze. Slivers of brilliant light knifed through the black shadows of dense forest. I climbed higher and higher up the slopes until I could see all the way down to the Rhine valley. I had no customers on this mountain track, but I walked on for the sheer pleasure of it. If I squinted hard enough, I could just barely make out the enormously tall spire of the Cathedral of Strasburg dissolving into the misty horizon.

Abruptly, my quiet contemplation was shattered. A large, ghostly gray dog sprinted out of the thick forest, planted its feet in the track right in front of me, and set up a terrible staccato barking. If I took a step forward, the dog's lips curled, its head sunk down between its shoulders, and a deep, throaty growl pinned me to my spot on the trail. I was trapped as surely as the unfortunate mice who snapped the traps in our cellar. I looked the hound straight in the eye, speaking softly. It was a beautiful creature, with glossy, short gray hair; long, loose ears; and a short-cropped tail that stood stiffly erect. It was clearly not a street mongrel but the product of generations of careful breeding.

Just as the dog calmed down, a gentleman came striding out of the forest. At first I imagined it was an apparition of my father. He seemed to be about fifty years old but still hale and vigorous. He was of medium height, slim and straight, with a robust, powerful build. His brown hair was streaked with gray and tousled into loose curls.

Everything about him exuded prosperity. His gray wool hunting costume was the finest quality—long, slim trousers of light gray worsted wool, with matching thigh-length coat, trimmed at the outer edges and around the pockets with black silk piping. His knee-high leather boots were polished to a perfection. As he opened his gun, separating the stock from the barrel so it would not accidentally discharge, his coat swung open revealing an ultramarine silk lining. He was clearly more than simply prosperous in the manner the Schultz family was prosperous. His clothing, his bearing, and fine hunting hound clearly displayed his high social stature.

I had never before encountered a patrician face-to-face. My words tripped over themselves as they tumbled over my tongue, falling out of my mouth in a knotted stammer. "I ...I ...am sorry. Your, your, hound. He was barking. I ...I ..." My face reddened, and I finally gave up trying to untangle my tongue.

He smiled indulgently. "I heard my dog. As you say, he was barking rather persistently. I thought he had found the doe we were hunting. And I see he was right." His eyes twinkled with amusement as a wry smile belied the intensity of his gaze.

"And what a pretty doe she is. What's your name, Fraulein." His eyes bored into me.

"I am Anastasia." I examined my scuffed shoes planted in the dirt track.

"Please, Anastasia, lift your head and look at me." He placed his index finger below my chin and gently tilted my head up. "Well, well!" He said, appraising me for whatever possibilities I might hold, as he might a new hunting dog.

"And what is in the basket you carry?"

"I …I …am a tailor, a dressmaker, and a seamstress. I was just delivering this to the Brauns'." I pointed vaguely over my shoulder.

Without asking my permission, he reached toward my basket with a well-manicured hand and uncovered it. He held up the inelegant bloomers within. "Ha, ha, ha. I see you are intimate with this family."

"No, no, sir. You misunderstand." I was simultaneously embarrassed and resentful that he should make me feel this way. I bristled visibly as I snatched the undergarments from his hand, replaced them in the basket, and pulled the corner of the towel back into place over the basket.

"I was just joking, my dear," he smiled. Then abruptly he changed the course of the conversation. "I am a visitor in this place. I am staying at the hunting lodge of my friend. I do not live here. Since I am on my own and do not know any local seamstresses, would you do me the honor of mending a few of my items that need repair?"

I was confused and uneasy. This situation was so unexpected and so unlikely to me that it hardly seemed real. I had no idea what was proper or how I should respond, so I hesitated.

"Are you unwilling to work for me then?" His tone darkened almost imperceptibly.

"No, no, of course not. I would be delighted to help you with your mending. I can also construct fine garments and work with the best fabrics of all types." My tongue untied itself, and I immediately began saying too much.

The smile returned to his eyes, which had never left my face. "Well then, follow me." He abruptly turned his back and strode confidently up a path I had never taken, to a place I had never been.

After few minutes' walk, I saw the hunting lodge. It was surrounded by such dense forest that it was no wonder I had never before seen it. The lodge had two stories, the lower of which was orange brick, a hue not made from our native soil. The upper story was half-timbered. The wooden double door was ornately carved and imbedded in a massive brick archway. Though the basic architecture was familiar, the scale was grand.

He grasped the huge brass ring on the door and pushed it open. The hall that received us was paneled from the floor to its twenty-foot ceiling in a lustrous dark oak. Fine sculptures of hounds, roe deer, and various wild animals were interspersed between the carved wooden benches lining the walls of the entryway. Above them the paneled walls were inlaid with fanciful mosaics made from various varieties and colors of wood arranged like an intricate puzzle of diamond shapes fitted tightly together to create a sunburst pattern. At our feet, the parquet floor was polished to a rich amber glow.

He led us into a smaller room off the great entry. "Please, make yourself comfortable." He invited me to take a seat on one of the rich, leather couches arranged around an enormous, marble hearth. I took a seat and glanced down. My feet rested on a woven rug that looked to me like the Persian rugs I had seen in books. Wooden wainscoting covered the lower part of the wall. Above it, dozens of heads of deer, boar, bear, and disembodied antlers covered the walls. Though the couch was deep and enveloping, I sat primly on its edge. I could not have been more uncomfortable.

"Tell me about yourself, Anastasia." His tone was at once very familiar and condescending. "Are you married?"

"No, sir. I am not married."

"Are you a virgin then?" He asked matter-of-factly, arching one eyebrow.

I cannot describe my shock at his question. My speechlessness returned. I could not control my breathing. I had an urge to flee this place immediately.

"I see by your reaction that you are not. It's just as well." He looked at me over the top of his hand lighting his pipe tobacco.

"I'm sorry sir, I must return to town. The Brauns will be expecting me." I rose to leave.

"Oh dear, I have frightened you, just like the doe we were chasing. Please sit down. Can you read, Anastasia? Have you ever seen a library?" He changed the subject so quickly that I was once again thrown into confusion.

"A library?" I don't know why my words came out as a question. Of course I had seen a library. My own father had accumulated a few generous shelves of books. And I knew Abraham Frankel must have hundreds.

"You know what a library is, don't you?" Now he was clearly patronizing me.

"Oh yes. I love to read. My Father bought many books before he died. I have read them all. Now I am rereading them, as I cannot …" I had not been able to buy new books for several years now. I no longer had money for such luxuries. I stopped my words, swallowing them before I once again said too much.

"Really? You are a reader? Well, follow me." Again he turned as a drill sergeant might and walked gracefully out of the trophy room, down the hall, and into another room. He fully expected me to follow without question.

"You see, Anastasia? Do you like it? What suits your fancy? Philosophy, history, novels?" His tone, and raised eyebrows indicated he did not expect me to know the difference.

I directed my gaze to hundreds of books stacked on shelves that reached from floor to ceiling. I turned slowly to take in the entire room. Every wall was lined with books. In the center of one wall, a magnificent, carved hearth beckoned the reader to sit beside the fire. I could imagine the gentry, free from the bonds of necessity, spending long evenings reading before the opulent fireplace. A tall ladder on a track of rollers hung from the top of each wall of shelves so one could access the topmost books. Rich leather couches and chairs arrayed themselves around the spacious room. Tall casement windows held diamond-shaped panes of glass divided by lead mullions. Soaring windows punctuated the thick walls of shelves. Upholstered window seats invited the reader to catch the sun's light as it streamed through the wavy, glass panes. What would it be like to have an endless supply of books? What kind of person accumulated such a treasure?

"I love history; the Romans interest me. But recently, I have become intrigued by the new concepts of Alexander von Humboldt. I believe he calls his ideas natural philosophy. I confess I also liked Johann Wolfgang von Goethe's melodrama about young Werther."

I could see surprise spread across his face. "Yes, of course, Anastasia. Come, take a look around." He smoothly erased the look of surprise from his face.

"I'm sorry, sir. I would really love to examine your friend's library, but did you have work for me to tend to?"

This broke the spell, and he snapped back to the business at hand.

"I will go find the garments I need to have mended. While I am gone, feel free to choose a book for yourself. When you return my mending to me, say in two weeks from today, you can return the book and examine the library for another." He left.

The great library smelled of rich leather, musty paper, and pine logs in the fireplace. I ran my fingers over the spines of red leather book covers, embossed with gold lettering. *The Republic, Apology, Phaedra* by Plato. These were books I had never heard of written in Greek. There was a book by von Humboldt I had heard was greatly praised, *Personal Narrative of Travels to the Equinoctial Regions of the New Continent During the Years 1799–1804.* I leafed through the pages of a book called *The Treasure Chest* by Johann Peter Hebel. It promised to be both humorous and enlightening. There were so many books that I felt light-headed. I stood in the grand library, Hebel's book laying open in my hands, and gazed up at shelves filled with more books than I had ever imagined. If I could live in this room and could roam my beloved hills, I would be happy for the rest of my life.

My host returned with fine undergarments, sleep tunics, and an intricate brocade smoking jacket with a torn crimson lining.

"I see you have found a book. Do you want to borrow that one?" He glanced at the book that lay open in my hands. I nodded absently. He led the way to the door.

"I trust you can find your way back home?" A gentleman, I thought, would have escorted me back down to the well-traveled trail.

"Yes, of course," I said, though I was not altogether sure I could do so in the waning light.

"I'll bring these back in two weeks then." I knew I would be back as long as he wanted me to come, if it meant I could borrow his friend's books.

"Yes, of course. I will see you then." He flicked his wrist as if dismissing a servant.

As I fumbled down the steep path from the lodge to the main track, I realized I did not know the man's name. I did not know anything about him. But he knew plenty about me. What had just happened? My mind and emotions swam in a stew of confusion.

For the next two weeks, as I worked on his exquisite garments, I struggled to sort out my feelings. Was I intrigued? Did I feel subtly menaced by the man? Was I thrilled to be on such personal terms with someone of such high rank? I exhausted myself trying to decipher the murmurings of my body and soul. I had not come close to sorting out my contradictory feelings in the two weeks I worked on his garments. The work seemed so personal, so intimate. I was anxious to show off my most skillful hand. But why did I even care what he thought? He both fascinated and repelled me. But oh, all those books! My memory could visualize the room in perfect detail, even to the extent of smelling the rich leather covers of the rare volumes.

Two weeks later, as promised, I made my way back up the hill. The knot in my chest was knit from strands of eager anticipation, dread, fear, and fascination. I pounded the door with the heavy, metal door knocker. There was no answer for a long time. I expected a servant to open the door. Surely he did not occupy the house without attendants. But the huntsman himself pulled the door open. He stood in the entry hall, elegant and relaxed in a deep blue velvet smoking jacket and loose pants pinched at the ankles, like I imagined an Arab sheik would wear.

"Come in, Anastasia. I see you remembered how to find me." Once again, I felt the intensity of his gaze.

"I have done the mending you requested. And here is the book I borrowed." I placed his neatly repaired, cleaned and folded garments on the entryway side table. More reluctantly, I lifted the book from my basket and held it out to him.

"How did you like it?" he inquired.

"Oh, it was a great pleasure to read," I enthused. "The stories were easy to read and funny. I believe he was writing of the people of Karlsruhe, but his observations are equally true of Gruntal." I flashed my brightest smile remembering the book's delightful anecdotes.

I fumbled with the basket, not knowing how to ask him for my pay.

124

We'd never talked about payment, but as enjoyable as the book was, it would not buy bread.

"I mended three items," I began, feeling as awkward as a cow on ice. "My usual fee would be—"

"Now, now, let's not ruin the moment by talking of money. You need not worry. Your efforts will be rewarded."

"I'm sorry, sir, but I must tend to my business. I cannot afford to work for the privilege of borrowing books." I stood my ground.

He fumbled in his pocket, withdrew as much money as I could earn in a month, and carelessly tossed it into my basket. His disdainful grimace showed his distaste for the financial transaction. I felt humiliated, but not for long.

"The library?" I ventured to mention the real reason I'd consented to come back.

"Of course, the library." In the manner that was becoming familiar to me, he turned on the heel of his soft, felt slippers and walked into that majestic garden of wisdom and learning.

"Please, Anastasia, take your time to look around. In this corner, you will find the histories. Didn't you tell me you enjoyed reading Roman history? Some of these books are very old and fragile. Please handle them with the utmost care." He stood back and studied me as I lost myself in this palace of reading pleasure.

I tentatively ran my fingers over the spines of books with titles in German, Latin, French, Greek, and languages I did not even recognize. My exploring fingers lingered over a book by a name I recognized—*Candide* by Voltaire. Gingerly I tipped the top edge of the book outward and slid it gently off the shelf.

"Oh, that one." My host intoned. "That is not actually a history. It more properly belongs either in works of fiction or philosophy. But the edition you are holding has been translated into German." He looked at the wonder in my face as I fanned through the gold-edged pages.

"You may enjoy reading that one if, as you say, you enjoyed *The Sorrows of Young Werther*. It has a similar theme. The protagonist indulges in a great deal of introspection and similarly becomes despondent and disillusioned. Would you like to take that one home with you?" he asked matter-of-factly.

I couldn't stop myself from opening to the first page, devouring the words as greedily as a starving person would ravage a chicken thigh. I was immersed in the lovely language. It took me a moment to sense his presence behind me, closer now. Out of the corner of my eye, I saw one arm on either side of my head, palms flattened against the wooden shelf. I felt energy radiate off of him. Startled, I spun around to see his face inches from mine. His eyes were slightly closed, his breathing was deep and regular. He was caught in a spell of his own, totally unrelated to the books. I drew a sharp breath. My impulse was to flee. But just as I had been trapped by the dog, I was now trapped by him. His arms and body became a cage that imprisoned me against the shelves. Abruptly, he pulled away. His face calmed and returned to normal. It was as if nothing had passed between us.

I wanted to run, but I was conflicted. I didn't want him to think me a fool, and I really wanted to take this treasure home. "May I still borrow the book?" I asked, as if I had done something wrong that needed his forgiveness.

"Yes, certainly, Anastasia. I will see you again in another week, after you have read it." Again he dismissed me with a flick of his wrist, as though I had suddenly become an annoyance.

With as much composure as I could muster, I turned and walked purposefully to the door without turning to look back at him. As I walked home, a sudden chill took my body and shook it. I couldn't tell if it was the fresh air of late autumn, fear, or shock. Could it possibly be desire? I didn't care. I had my book. I resolved not to think of the whole encounter again.

It was frightening on so many levels. Again I felt slightly menaced. But I was also powerfully attracted. To what? To his wealth? No, I could not believe I was so shallow. Was I attracted to the mystery of the man, the house, the unlikely events that led me to this place? Yes, I thought, that was it. But in my heart I knew it was more. I was attracted to him as a woman, plain and simple. I had not felt like a desirable woman in so long. Now I did.

One week later, I set out again to the elegant lodge hidden in the depths of the dark forest. My hand no longer trembled as I hefted the heavy door knocker. I waited with staunch resolve, determined to do what was necessary to make another withdrawal from his library. I was, as he pointed out, not a virgin. These visits were unknown to anyone but the two of us. I resigned myself to his intentions. I was so busy earning a living, I had never considered that I might miss the affections of a man. Now, I could imagine rekindling the ember of desire I had long ago abandoned.

My visits continued for six more weeks. At the beginning of November, the weather took an inevitable turn toward winter. A light snow had fallen. The trails were slick in the shady spots and muddy in the sunny spots. By the time I reached the door knocker, my skirts and shoes were spattered. Mud streaked my legs beneath my skirts.

"My dear, Anastasia, look at you." His laugh was gentle, but his eyes smoldered.

"Here is the book I borrowed. What do you suggest this time?" I tried my best to sound like we were making a simple business transaction.

"Look at you," he repeated. "Let's get you cleaned up."

He led me up the stairs to an elegant four-poster bed, so high it required a step stool to mount. Gently, in the full light of day, he removed my skirt. He carefully stroked each leg in turn, as he intently ran a wet towel down each one from thigh to ankle.

"There, now. You are beautiful again." He dropped the wet towel and rose to face me. He brought his face close to mine and kissed me. I did not close my eyes. I saw my own image reflected in his eyes. For the first time in a very long time, I felt beautiful.

He took me with thoughtful patience. He did not rush and was as attentive to my pleasure as he was to his own. Our encounter was wordless, yet frank. It was nothing like my wholehearted, innocent, ardent first love with Rupert. Nor was it like the greedy, passionate heat I felt for Matthias. This love was unexpected and satisfying, born not of neediness or lust but of loneliness and tenderness.

When our encounter had run its course, he abruptly changed the subject in his inimitable way. "Let's go back to the library. I have something special for you." He pirouetted and, with his back to me, pulled his elegant Turkish robe around him. I struggled back into my muddy, wet clothes and followed him. He picked up a beautifully bound book from the library desk.

"*The Hunchback of Notre Dame* by Alexandre Dumas." I read the name in a whisper and looked up at him quizzically.

"This was specially translated into German. It is the only volume of its kind not in French. I hope you will enjoy it. May it keep you warm on the coming winter nights." He placed the book in my hands, leaned forward, and tenderly kissed my forehead.

"Does this mean I am not meant to come back here anymore?" I was surprised and disappointed that we would not continue to meet. But then, what did I think? That we had a future together? Certainly not!

Then, for the last time, he turned his back and led me to the grand entrance hall. "My dear Anastasia. I hope our brief entanglement will be as pleasant a memory for you as it will be for me." He opened the door.

I walked through and then turned and stood facing him. Leaning his back against the heavy door, he closed it.

Sometimes life gives us an unexpected gift. I left that day feeling well loved. I could have said no to this gift, and though that might have been the proper thing to do, I desired the book almost as much as I desired him. But the warmth in my heart and the precious book in my hand told me I was right to accept the gift life had offered me.

I never saw his face again. I never knew his name, but he was right. I would not forget him.

CHAPTER 11

THE FOUNDLING

1839

As autumn died into winter, morning sickness, lethargy, and constant hunger took hold, and new life stirred within me. I knew there would be another baby by summer.

I'd thought my age would have precluded any chance of conception, but I was wrong. I should have felt angry or humiliated. I should have felt guilty or embarrassed. I should have been remorseful. Somehow, I felt none of these emotions. It is hard to describe what I felt.

I was forty-three years old—old enough to understand the consequences of my actions. I should have known better. My short interlude could have been the subject of a romantic tragedy like those in the books I loved to read. But what I felt was a gauzy euphoria, as if someone had sprinkled fairy dust over me or a magic genie had granted me the gift of one last love, a gift I'd never wished for nor imagined. During my time with the huntsman, it was as if I had been living someone else's life, a fictional life of sensual pleasure ensconced in opulence, not my own life of struggle and worry. This child, fathered by an anonymous stranger, would be a child conceived of a simple love that made no demands and had no expectations.

I hid my condition as long as possible. I left the shop on my rounds very early each morning, before it was fully light and when the prying eyes of the townspeople were barely opening. I held my sewing basket in front of me and swathed my body in a loose cloak that hid my form. The few people who observed me saw only a familiar shape in a hooded cape, clutching her basket of mending, winding her way through side streets and mountain tracks.

Even when the summer heat made it uncomfortable, I concealed myself in my cloak and loose-fitting housedresses. My face did not grow plump and rosy; my hair did not grow lush and shiny; only my stomach expanded. My clients took my visits for granted. Often, I interacted only with the housemaid. Because I was largely invisible to them anyway, it was not too difficult to keep my condition a secret. So I carried on as usual.

Francisca took care of shopping, cooking, gardening, and the housework, as she had always done. I had no need to be seen in the market or at the bakery, at the festivals, or out on the streets. The dress form with my custom-designed dress disappeared from the display, discouraging visitors to the shop.

Francisca, of course, noticed my condition. "Who did this to you?" she demanded with righteous indignation.

"I cannot say," I demurred.

"But you must know the man. What do you mean, you cannot say?" Loyal Francisca was willing to attribute all blame on the father of this child, as if I was an innocent bystander.

"Yes, I knew the man, but he is gone now," I replied in low tones.

"What do you mean, 'gone now'? Where did he go? Anyway, if he is gone now, then there is no harm in telling me his name."

"I cannot name him." I mumbled.

"Anastasia, please. This is madness. Just tell me who the father is." Francisca's voice was pleading and frustrated in equal measure.

"I cannot name him because I did not know his name. I know it sounds like madness, Francisca. I know! He was an aristocrat, a rich man—someone of very high social status. We met by accident as I was on my mountain route. We met a few times. That is all I know of him."

"Is that where those richly bound books came from?" she said gesturing toward the bedroom. "I wondered how you ever found enough money to buy such things." Francisca was red-faced and agitated.

"Yes, the books were gifts, as is this child. Please be happy for me. This child might be a blessing and a comfort to us. Won't it be good to have a child's laughter and lively energy in our house once again?" I tried to put the best face on my predicament, which, in fact, would be Francisca's predicament too.

"Anastasia! You must be suffering some mental defect! How will we ever explain another baby in the house? Neither of us is married or even associating with any of the men in town. You know how people talk." She continued. "Both of us could lose all our customers. I can easily see Frau Stein lifting her chin, crossing to the other side of the street, and walking as fast her stout legs would carry her. Can you think of a single person who would accept this situation?" Francisca was the voice of reason, pulling me from my world of fantasy and denial.

"I don't know what we'll do. I don't know. I will think of something." She was right, of course. I needed to think of some way the baby would not suffer the same indignities that Peter Paul had suffered—called a bastard by anyone wishing to bully him. This time, it would be worse. This baby would seem totally inexplicable. I could never admit that I'd had an assignation with a mysterious stranger. It would sound like I was losing my sanity. And if anyone believed the truth, it would make me seem little more than a whore. Despite the lush pleasure I had enjoyed with the baby's father, I knew I was no whore. My feelings about myself had not changed. I still saw myself as the proud, strong-willed girl I had been at sixteen.

Plans and schemes haunted my dreams. My first thought was that I could give the baby to an orphanage. No, I could never do that. I could find a childless couple and give the baby to them. Maybe I could even visit it from time to time. But I didn't know of any, and besides, that could never be kept secret. That was only another fantasy. Dozens of schemes came and went in my mind. All were impossible, or at the very least impractical. And all of them involved losing my baby so someone else's care. Finally I rejected all of them.

By the time summer arrived, I had devised a plan. It was almost as impossible as all the others, but if this plan worked I would be able to keep my baby. It was a terrible risk, but Francisca agreed to help.

Alex was born on a balmy summer night in July. Francisca and I had chosen the name many months ago. When the pains began, I kept my peace and did not cry out. Francisca attended me, though she knew little of the birthing process. The pains began in early evening. As they overtook me, making even speech difficult, I instructed Francisca. Terrified though she was, she focused on her task and did exactly as I told her.

The laboring was mercifully short. It was an easy birth, if any birth can be called easy. The baby swam out of my body facing backward, head first, without the cord wrapped around his neck. And then it was done. Alexius had entered our lives.

The baby looked so much like Father, it was startling. He was small but solid, perfectly well formed in every detail, with wispy, brown curls. He had the same long lashes my little lost Alouysius had had.

I held Alex to my heart and kissed him. All the tenderness and love that had been sequestered away in my heart for years found a home in this little baby. I thought no mother on earth had ever loved a baby more than I loved this beautiful, inexplicable sprout. We spent one day and one night in bed, almost as physically close as we were before his birth. I looked into his eyes; stroked his perfect skin, as soft as any satin fabric I had ever touched; and examined every small detail of his body, drinking him in as he drank from me. During that day of recovery, I steeled my nerves to carry out our plan.

In the morning, I gave him to Francisca. Francisca was terrified but determined to see it through. In the early hours of morning, before sunrise, before the town came to life, she draped a long, gray, hooded cloak around her. Carefully bundling the sleeping newborn into a basket, she made her way down the side streets and alleys and deposited the basket on the steps of St. Michael's Church. She left him there and returned home. We waited together at home for the first streaks of pale ochre to paint the horizon.

In a little while, he demanded to be fed in the only way a baby can. From my bedroom window, I could hear him wailing. My body responded viscerally, with a will of its own. Though the morning air at my bedroom window stroked my face with damp and cool fingers, sweat rolled down. My still-tender womb contracted painfully, and the milk that had just begun to flow responded to his urgent need. Wet stains circled my breasts. Drops of the pale liquid dropped onto my lap. It took all the strength of will I possessed not to run to him. For every one of his cries, I cried a hundred tears. What if someone else found him first? We wanted people to hear him but be addled by sleep and slow to react. What if some feral animal found him? Suddenly our plan seemed the most foolish thing a mother had ever done. I was dizzy with anxiety.

As dawn broke, Francisca hefted her basket of vegetables and walked toward St. Michael's as she would on any market day, as always wanting to be the first person to set up shop. When she arrived at the church steps, she laid siege to the rectory door until she roused the pastor's housekeeper. Francisca's urgent anxiety was as real as mine. She ardently begged to be allowed to take the foundling she had just discovered on the church steps to our home. We had carefully rehearsed every possible reason we should take him to our home. We were ready to say we had room for him. We were capable of taking care of him. The baby needed to be cared for right now. Listen to him. He's hungry. We live close by and can attend to his immediate needs without waiting and making the baby suffer hunger longer than necessary. We were two lonely old spinsters and would be the best people to keep him until his mother could be found.

For me, the hour between when she left with her basked of vegetables and when she returned with the swaddled, still screaming infant might as well have been a year. Finally, as the cool, dewy dawn warmed into a warm July morning, she returned. She had abandoned her basket of vegetables on the church steps. In its place, she carried the baby, our baby. His face was red with infant outrage. He kicked his blankets aside and roared.

"Alex, oh my Alex! You've come home!" I embraced his tiny body.

"There will be an inquest," Francisca breathlessly announced. "They let me take him home, but it was a struggle to convince them. They are going to look for any girl who might have left this baby on the church stairs." Her face was almost as flushed as baby Alex's.

"Francisca, you are my savior." I put the baby down and embraced my sister with all my heart.

"It was a terrible risk we took. The pastor and his housekeeper nearly did not let me take him. They were going to give him to the nuns. I had to use almost every argument we prepared to convince them. And he is not yet ours. They might still take him from us." Her voice was husky with anxiety. She was as inflamed as I had ever seen her.

"I agreed to return to have him baptized this afternoon," Francisca concluded. Pressing for an immediate baptism was part of our plan. We would have my name on the official baptismal record. If no one claimed the baby, it would be our evidence of adoption.

Late in the afternoon, the three of us, Francisca, baby Alex, and I, returned to the rectory for the simple ceremony. I answered the questions the pastor intoned:

"What name do you give to this baby?"

"Alexius Burkart."

"What do you ask of God's church for Alexius Burkart?"

"Baptism."

"You have asked to have your child baptized. In doing so, you are accepting the responsibility of training him in the practice of the faith. It will be your duty to bring him up to keep God's commandments, by loving God and our neighbor as Christ taught us. Do you clearly understand what you are undertaking?"

"I do."

Turning to Francisca, the godmother, he said "Are you ready to help the parent of this child in her duty to be a Christian parent?"

"I am."

"Do you renounce Satan?"

"I do."

"And all his works?"

"I do."

"And all his empty promises?"

"I do."

"Do you believe in God, the Father Almighty, creator of heaven and earth?"

"I do."

The priest dribbled water over Alex's head, dipped his thumb in holy oil, and made the sign of the cross on his forehead. "I baptize you in the name of the Father, the Son, and the Holy Spirit."

"Amen."

And so it went. Francisca, as Alex's sponsor, vowed to care for his immortal soul if I could not. The cadence of the ancient ritual comforted us. For the first time in three days, we were able to breathe again.

I filled out the paperwork:

Baby's name: Alexius Burkart
Mother: Anastasia Burkart

Father: unknown
Grandfather: Anton Burkart
Grandmother: Maria Anna Stehle

When the words of the sacrament had been uttered and the ink had dried on my son's baptismal certificate, the pastor turned to us with a stern warning. "You understand that we will look for the mother. He is only yours until we find her. We can change the church record at that time." His stern words of warning flew past us as benignly as summer butterflies.

"We understand. But now we know his soul is secure, and he will not be banished to limbo without the blessing of baptism should he die. We will raise him as our own for as long as he is in our care," I proclaimed, trying to show as little emotion as possible.

Time passed, and no mother was found.

We no longer had anything to hide. Pangs of terror softened into grateful relief. By telling and retelling the story of the foundling, it became real to everyone, even to ourselves. As the months passed, we carefully introduced him as our foundling son and then simply as our son. Anxiety loosened its grip as a boa constrictor gives up squeezing its prey.

CHAPTER 12

BACK TO SCHOOL

1844–1846

When the bright tone of the bell over the door chimed, I lifted my eyes from my mending. The sound of the bell buoyed my spirits as it always had, kindling anticipation that something good was coming into my life—new business, a friendly face, important news. This day, it was Peter who entered the shop. Peter did not often come to visit. Nor did he confide in me. He was deeply attached to the Schultz family, who relied on him to bear much of the responsibility for their farm. So it was a surprise when he showed up at our door on a balmy Saturday evening in early autumn. I dropped my mending and rose to greet him, arms outstretched.

He returned my embrace. He was now twenty-one years old, a full grown man. He was, like his father, tall, erect, and muscular. His arms engulfed my entire body and pressed me into his chest. I buried my face into the coarse linen of his shirt, still redolent with the smell of grape vines. My head grazed his chin.

"Peter! I am so happy to see you. Please. Sit down. Better yet, let's go upstairs to the kitchen. Francisca will be delighted to see you too. I'm sure she can make a cup of kaffee for you. I think she baked apples today. You'll need something to nourish you after your long walk into town." I effervesced with the surprise.

He followed me up the stairs without a word.

"Peter!" Francisca bubbled. "What a nice surprise. Come, sit down. I'll warm these baked apples for you."

When he was comfortably seated, with his hands wrapped around a steaming kaffee cup and the irresistible smell of apples baked with honey and cinnamon rising from the plate before him, I finally gave voice to my curiosity. "What brings you here? You are always welcome, of course, but we are usually the ones to come up to the Schultz's home to visit you. Do you have some important news for us?"

"Well, you see, winter is coming," he began, looking straight at the plate in front of him, twisting his napkin in his strong fists.

"Yes, I suppose so, though it doesn't feel much like impending winter this evening, does it?" Honey-colored light filtered in through the open windows, and a comforting, warm breeze gently stirred Francisca's lace curtains.

"I'm a grown man now. Many young men my age are becoming skilled craftsmen or working at the new factories and coal mines in Essen. They will be independent someday soon and free to build lives of their own." He finally looked up at me and Francisca, who sat calmly at my side.

Neither Francisca nor I spoke, but waited with eyebrows raised anticipating further explanation.

"Yes, independent. Well, I cannot see a future for me with the Schultz farm. Clem and Hilda's oldest son, Heinrich, is now twelve, the age I was when I started working for them. Soon enough, he will be groomed to take over the farm, leaving me with no path forward." His eyes were intense. Two small, vertical worry lines indented the space between his eyes. He waited for a response.

I did not speak immediately. In truth, I had never thought of Peter's aspirations. I hadn't realized he was ambitious, not satisfied to be a "hired hand" all his life. I was so accustomed to the security the Schultz family provided him that my son's future had never caused me a moment's worry.

Francisca spoke first. "Dear Peter," she began warmly, "you have clearly given this a lot of thought. What did you have in mind?"

"As I said, winter is coming. I have heard of a school in Lichtenfels that teaches the newest techniques in basket making. In particular, they are weaving very stout baskets of peeled willow that are now being used in the coal mines. I would like to travel there this winter to study the craft."

"But don't farmers weave their own baskets?" I wondered.

"Yes, they have traditionally done so, but the school is teaching a new technique that produces very strong, rugged baskets for industrial use. You need strong hands to make them." He held up his hands. They did indeed look strong. Callouses lined his palms, hardened by years of physical labor, with long, tapered fingers and nails edged all around with dirt. You could see sinews rise and fall with the movement of each finger.

"And the world is changing, Mama. The ironworks in the Ruhr River valley need coal. The new railway between Dresden and Leipzig runs on coal. Small farmers are failing and farmers are leaving their farms to work in the factories in the north, or they are looking for work as laborers on other farms. Many of them are losing the craft of basket weaving." Clearly Peter had planned his arguments. His reasoning was sound. I suddenly saw Peter's future from his own point of view. What had seemed like a rich opportunity working with Clem Schultz had become a dead end, a trap that would keep him forever dependent on his employer indefinitely.

"I see no problem with learning a new craft. Do you, Francisca?" I asked, glancing at Francisca as she stared intently at Peter.

"Well you see, there is a bit of a problem," Peter continued. "Herr Schultz has been paying me a small amount since I was sixteen. I'm sure you remember that, in the years between when I was twelve and sixteen, I worked for only room and board, plus the experience and knowledge Herr Schultz shared with me. But now that I am being paid, I must pay for room and board. I have managed to save very little money." He dropped his voice and turned the kaffee mug in front of him around and around in its saucer. "I was wondering if you could loan me enough to pay my expenses over the winter." His voice was so quiet I wasn't sure if I had heard him correctly.

Without a word, Francisca and I looked at each other, eyebrows raised. "Peter, we are just barely providing for ourselves." My voice did not mask my surprise.

Francisca laid a hand on my forearm, signaling me to stop. "Dear Peter. Of course we will help you. How much do you need?" she answered without a moment's hesitation.

"Have you asked Clem if he can spare you? Have you discussed this plan with him?" My voice sounded harsh. I felt shamed by my selfishness.

"Yes, Mama, I have." His face grew red. His eyes seemed to sink a bit into their sockets. "He said that he could spare me for one winter. Since there will be less to do in that season, he said it would be a good time for him to introduce young Heinrich to the workings of the farm. But he will not pay me my wages during my absence or fund my schooling." Ah, so there was the real issue. I could see it embarrassed Peter to need our financial help after working for so many years.

"Don't worry, Peter. Francisca and I will find a way." I sounded more confident than I felt. In truth, I had no idea how we would magically produce the extra money. "I completely understand your desire to be an independent man, with your own path to tread." I said this in all sincerity. Hadn't I been pursuing my own independence since I was the young tailor's apprentice?

"I know you understand, Mama. And I know life has been a struggle for you since Grosspapa died. But I will repay you, I promise. I just need help getting a start." Peter breathed a heavy sigh. His back straightened as if a great burden had been lifted from it.

I could hear the door slam downstairs. Little Alex, now a lively five-year-old, came bounding up the stairs. "Peter! What are you doing here? Come on, let's play hide-and-seek! I've found all the best hiding places in the whole house. You'll never find me!" Little Alex was beaming.

The spell of our serious conversation was broken. A smile blossomed on Peter's somber face. He grabbed one of Alex's arms and one of his ankles in his strong hands and pivoted around, swinging Alex in big circles. Alex extended his free arm and leg out as he "flew" through the air, laughing with abandon.

Francisca and I sat at the table. I reached out and touched her wrist. We looked at each other and then at the boys—our "big boy," now a young man, and our foundling son, a solid, energetic boy with a precocious intelligence—as they laughed and played. I sighed deeply. Misty eyes blurred the sight of my sons, happy brothers.

That night, I went to bed filled with anxiety. Our options were limited. I could redouble my efforts to find new customers. Francisca could try to grow more produce and maybe find buyers in the market for her tatting. Somehow, we would find a way.

The summers of 1845 and 1846 were unseasonably cool and rainy. Crops either failed completely, or harvests were greatly reduced. Similar weather in Ireland caused an unparalleled disaster. The news from Ireland was staggering. The *Freiburg Gazette* described total failure of the potato crop. Potatoes rotted in the ground. Those that were dug up were shriveled, corky, and reeked with a smell never to be forgotten. In Ireland, by the second year of the failure, hundreds of thousands of peasant farmers starved to death. In our beautiful land of the Schwarzwald, we lost most of our potatoes as well, and much of our rye and barley. Not since 1817, "the year with no summer," when rain poured down incessantly, the skies turned a dirty tan, and the summer stayed much cooler than normal, had we experienced a crop failure like this one. Then, as now, destitute farmers begged from door to door, dug through trash heaps, and stole whatever was not tied down.

Francisca had difficulty keeping the soil in her well-tended garden drained well enough to prevent rot. She resorted to protecting her precious crop by covering it with burlap. With widespread scarcity, it was even more important for Francisca to persevere. We came to rely more and more on Francisca's income. Her diligence was rewarded with a good crop. The produce she saved from the dreadful weather fetched higher prices in the market as farmers' offerings dwindled.

Even the prosperous Schultz farm suffered. To Clem's credit, his farm never relied on only one crop, so while some of the barley and rye yields were greatly reduced, the leafy greens thrived. The grapes suffered but still produced a reduced but important harvest. His cows, pigs, and chickens continued to be well fed and to provide food and income for the family's needs.

After Peter's autumn visit but before the snow closed the roads, he traveled on the post route to Lichtenfels. His letters home that winter were filled with wonder and excitement at seeing a world beyond the fields, forests, and farms of home:

> Dear Mama and Aunt Mausi,
>
> It took me three weeks to arrive on the post carriage. I never imagined how wide the world is. I am staying at a hostel shared by twenty-five other young men, here to seek their fortunes or learn a trade. I have met many new friends. My funds do not allow me to go out to the beer halls and carouse around the town with the others, but I

do not feel deprived. It gives me more time to practice and perfect my technique.

You will be proud to know that I have not yet missed Sunday Mass. This is not as easy as it is at home, as this is a Lutheran country, and Catholic churches are few.

On the third Friday of each month, basket makers come from all over the area to display and sell their baskets. The variety and artistry of these masterful creations is far beyond anything we see in our town. My head is brimming with ideas for new designs.

The school is completely devoted to teaching the art of weaving baskets for every purpose. You will be proud of me when I return and show you how well I have spent my time. I cannot thank you, Mama and dear Tante Mausi, enough. I promise I will repay you with my eternal gratitude. Not only that, but my baskets will allow me to repay you with taler as well. I see a new future opening before me.

Your loving son,
Peter Paul Burkart

While my serious Peter attended to his studies, Francisca and I redoubled our efforts to produce enough extra income for his expenses. Ironically, the poor weather and meager crops worked to Francisca's advantage. The skills she'd gained through many years of nurturing her garden and her single-minded devotion to her harvest bore abundant fruit. Her prized vegetables far surpassed most of the other vendors, and her diligence was richly rewarded.

I made a list of every customer I'd ever served and visited each one, trekking all my old routes and soliciting dressmaking work. I designed three new dresses for the fortunate wives of the banker, the goldsmith, and Frau Greiser, whose mill had expanded to include metalwork. We took our successes as a sign that we were right in supporting Peter's education as best we could.

I swallowed my pride and visited Herr Baumgartner. His tailor shop, which had once stood on the edge of town, was now surrounded by new buildings. I straightened my spine, lifted my chin, and turned the handle on the shop door. Two apprentices sat cross-legged on the tailor's study table, stitching fervently. His clever rolling shelves were crowded with fabrics of every variety. He stocked machine-made cotton from the textile mills, silks from France, and even velvet for the wealthiest clients.

"Well, Frau Burkart, I'm surprised to see you." He smiled benignly. "I'm happy you have paid me a visit. It has been a long time since last I saw you," he continued in a cordial tone. "How have you and your family been faring in this austere time?" He seemed genuinely concerned.

The redness moving up my neck to my cheeks to my ears betrayed my humiliation. I tried my utmost not to sound desperate. "Good afternoon, Herr Baumgartner." I straightened my shoulders. The frayed hems and sleeves of my dress, though stylish in its time, showed its age. No matter, I would do what was necessary for my Peter. "I see you are very busy. I am here to see if I could help you. If you ever have more than your tailors can handle, or if you have seamstress jobs, I would like to offer my services. I still design dresses, when there is a call for it." I stood quietly, trying to maintain a shred of dignity.

Herr Baumgartner cocked his head and blinked at me. Clearly my offer had surprised him. "You see," he said, sweeping his arm out to encompass his busy shop, "I have several apprentices and all the help I need." He paused and seemed to reconsider his words.

Before he could continue, I blundered on. "Herr Baumgartner," I hesitated. "Do you remember my son, Peter? Well, he is currently in Lichtenfels at a school renowned for teaching basket weaving. Francisca and I are saving every taler we can to help him in his endeavor." I stopped short, not wishing to say more.

"I occasionally have a woman whose taste in dresses is beyond my abilities." This was an amazingly candid admission from one as successful as he, and I was not sure I believed him.

"Of course, I would treat any woman you referred to me with my very best service," I replied. "And I promise not to solicit any further work from her or her family. I would respect her as your customer. You can trust me in that."

"I believe you, Fraulein Burkart. I know your reputation. You are as honest as your father was known to be. I'll see what I can do."

We shook hands as two men would, as equals. As I turned to go, the breath I didn't realize I was holding escaped from my lungs. I felt at once deflated and grateful, humbled by the exchange but vindicated by the result.

* * *

When Peter returned, his enthusiasm for his new craft had endowed him with an energy I had never seen in him before.

"Will you return to Schultz's farm?" I asked.

"I promised Herr Schultz I would continue to work for him, though I don't know how much longer he will need me. I will now be tutoring young Heinrich. Sooner or later, he will no longer need my help. But I have a plan. During the evenings and next winter, I will create as many baskets as I can. Maybe you and Aunt Mausi can help me sell them in the market."

"Of course we will," Francisca enthused.

Peter plied his new trade with all the seriousness and diligence of a cloistered monk dedicated to saving souls with his prayers. He planted a special variety of willow wands in the moist fens along the stream above Herr Greiser's mill. They were more pliable and less brittle than the native variety. He wove them into masterful creations that were both decorative and practical. The baskets normally available at market during these years were simple basics. Most people could not afford ornamental basketry imported from other areas. But Peter's baskets were homegrown and crafted right here in Gruntal, so they were surprisingly affordable. We displayed samples of each of Peter's baskets. They were well-appreciated novelties, cleverly designed and expertly crafted.

He was right about his strong hands. He mastered the difficult craft of producing tall, cylindrical baskets that could be strapped to the backs of workers. Miners from across the Rhine at Saar to the Ruhr Valley in the north used this type of basket to haul coal out of mines.

I began accompanying Francisca to the market, bringing examples of my finer work to display to passersby, hoping to attract new customers from beyond the familiar lanes and paths.

During the spring of 1846, I noticed Francisca's behavior changing. Every market day, Francisca dressed with a bit more care. She brushed her glossy, long, honey-colored curls to a fine sheen. She wore a wide-brimmed, peasant-style hat that cast dark shadows over her face. She seemed more nervous than normal. After a few weeks, I learned her secret. A respectable-looking older gentleman, with dark brown hair fringed with gray at the temples and a fine gray streak running from forehead to crown visited Francisca's vegetable display every week. He spent an inordinate amount of time examining the vegetables. He spoke to Francisca in the formal tone of a schoolteacher. Francisca, now forty-one, was not accustomed to the attentions of men. But I recognized his interest for what it was, and it was not the vegetables that attracted him.

One day, I excused myself from Francisca and followed the gentleman at a discreet distance. When we were out of earshot of the market, I approached him and gently touched his elbow. "I'm really sorry to startle you, but I noticed you visit Francisca and myself with some regularity."

"I need to buy food, don't I?" he replied a bit defensively.

"Yes, of course. I don't mean to be forward, but may I ask your name?"

"Certainly. I am Ignaz Dilger."

"This is awkward for both of us, and I apologize for being so forward, but Francisca has no other family but me to look out for her. She is not sophisticated about the attentions of men ..." I trailed off.

"There is no need to apologize. I understand your concern. Let me introduce myself properly. I am a widower. My wife of twenty-five years died a few years ago. I find myself missing her terribly and crave companionship. I have observed Francisca for over a year, and I have never heard her utter a cross word to anyone or display the slightest impatience. She has a rare quality of serenity that I find irresistible. I admire her greatly."

"Are you asking my permission to keep company with her then?" I knew that I was jumping ahead, but we were not young people, and I felt candor was the best course in this situation.

"I would welcome the opportunity to become better friends with both of you," Herr Dilger said with a slight bow.

Herr Dilger's attentions were the very last thing Francisca expected. She warmed to him in the stuttering manner of a shy girl. Ignaz Dilger doted on her, and Francisca did everything in her power to make a good impression—cooking luscious meals, curling her hair, pinching her cheeks to give them a rosy color.

* * *

The following spring, when the plum blossoms shed their petals like a soundless, gentle rain, Francisca and Ignaz were wed in a simple ceremony. Francisca was every bit the blushing bride; I created a simple but elegant dress for my sister as I had done when she was a young girl. Two dozen creamy, tightly spaced satin buttons cascaded down the bodice from its neckline to its hem. A skirt, of the same fabric, billowed out from the bodice in generous soft folds. Bride and groom walked slowly, arm in arm, down the aisle of the old church as a few friends, Peter, Alex, and I looked on. Francisca carried salt and bread as an omen for good harvests, and Ignaz carried grain for wealth and good fortune.

After the wedding, the bride and groom boarded a fine carriage and left for Ignaz's home in Offenburg. As happy as I was for her, I could not imagine my life without her. Alex and I shared the house in which I had lived every day of my life. It was the same house, but everything was different. I filled my book of days with all the confidences I would have shared with Francisca. I struggled to grow vegetables, cook, clean, do laundry, and care for an active, growing boy entirely by myself, while still taking in mending and struggling to maintain the shop. Alex, with his schoolboy energy, splashed brightness into my life. But there were dark corners where blackness lurked. I knew I would desperately miss my sister's calm presence. Never had I felt so lonely.

CHAPTER 13

THE TROUBLES

1848

T he smell of cabbage and caraway permeated the kitchen. Alex and I were grateful that tonight we would have the fat Thuringian *rostbratwurst* that Francisca had bought for us at the market. Cabbage was one of the vegetables that forgave my poor gardening efforts. I was not much of a gardener, but I could coax the sturdier varieties to maturity. Root vegetables did not require too much time, and they could be stored in the cellar for months. So, cabbage and its sisters, Brussels sprouts, cauliflower, and radishes, would tolerate a little neglect. But our diet was much less varied and interesting than it had been when Francisca had lived with us.

Francisca had been radiant the previous day when she'd visited. Her marriage to Ignaz brought more fullness to her life than either of us could have imagined. When I'd first met him in the market, I'd thought Ignaz sounded like a schoolteacher. There was a good reason I got that impression. He taught composition, literature, and elocution at the gymnasium in Offenburg. His formal manner belied his generous, sympathetic nature.

Ignaz gave Francisca a new family, two grown daughters and one grown son, all well-educated, gainfully employed, and within a one- or two-day carriage ride from Offenburg. So, family visits were relatively easy. Ignaz's children treated Francisca with courtesy, not affection, but that was to be expected. They, like Ignaz, still mourned their mother's passing but accepted Francisca for their father's sake. Francisca never expected to displace their mother's memory and happily cultivated respectful, cordial relationships with her new family. She was delighted to inherit four grandchildren, lively, intelligent sprouts ranging between two and eight years old. The younger ones had no memory of their oma and embraced Francisca, who, at forty-three, was old enough to be treated like their grandmother.

The couple lived in the oldest section of town, just a few blocks from the gymnasium where Ignaz taught. The school was housed in a stately old building that had been a Benedictine monastery for centuries. His house was almost as old as the monastery but was warmed by coal-burning heaters in each room, lit with gas lamps, and filled with practical furnishings that hinted at moderate elegance. It was comfortable, clean, and spacious. Ignaz kept his housekeeper on after he married Francisca, a luxury she had never imagined.

His sympathetic nature allowed him to see that, though she was growing to love him in a deeply companionable way, she also pined for those she left behind. Offenburg would have been a two- or three-day journey by the network of footpaths that joined the many small towns. Even riding the post route carriage would have required an overnight stay at one of the roadhouses. But the year Francisca was married, train service began between our towns, making it much easier for us to see each other. He did not begrudge her the monthly train trips she took to visit us. She always brought us practical gifts that were well appreciated. We strolled, arm in arm, through the market, Francisca chatting with her old friends and I discreetly scanning the crowd for potential customers.

Alex and I lived in such austerity now that we were grateful for whatever she could offer us. Our house was less clean and orderly than it had been when Francisca cared for us. Our clothes were old but as well maintained as I could keep them. My books—even the books Alex's father had given me—were time-worn and dog-eared as they looked down at us from their shelf in the parlor. The areas in the garden that Francisca had cultivated in graceful orderliness now sprouted weeds, and unwanted volunteer plants overran the perimeters with abandon.

Alex helped by doing his chores, including what would normally be "woman's work"—washing dishes and the laundry. He did not complain. But I begrudged every hour he spent on housekeeping. He was so brightly intelligent that he deserved better than what I could give him. Though only nine years old, he excelled at declamation and could recite long passages of classic poetry like Schiller's *Das Lied von der Glocke* (*The Song of the Bell*). At school, he was the boy who always made excellence look easy and very seldom suffered slapped knuckles for not mastering his Latin lessons.

He had a restless spirit, always eager to pursue his next adventure. His enthusiasms were intense, but short-lived. After a short time, a week or a month, instead of capturing snakes and insects by the river (or whatever his most recent passion had been) he would become engrossed in building small boats out of fallen limbs and making sails out of linen scraps from the shop.

Alex was small in stature and sturdily built. He had lively eyes and capable, short-fingered hands. A fringe of dark curls framed his wide face. Vigorously healthy, he seldom caught so much as a cold. In this, he was one of the lucky ones.

All around us, peasant children suffered from the ills that poverty brought to their families—chronic coughs, red eyes oozing with infection, and lice crawling through their uncombed hair. Many farmers, dispossessed of their lands because crop failure had made it impossible for them to pay their landlord's rent, wandered the streets begging in the markets, sometimes even picking the pockets of distracted shoppers. Dysentery, one of the many scourges the wandering poor endured, was rife among them.

Compared to their lot, we fared well. My response to the widespread suffering was to put all other thoughts aside and work with renewed fervor. I visited Herr Baumgartner every week, soliciting whatever work he could give me. I worked every day, even Sunday, catching up on housework and gardening. I struggled to maintain my equilibrium while turbulence rocked my little boat of safety. There was a restive atmosphere all around us.

Since the State of Baden joined the Zollverein in 1836, the grand duke had instituted several liberal reforms. It seemed our region of Baden was moving toward freedom from the medieval system of fiefdoms and aristocratic privilege. But by 1848, the spark of revolution reignited in France and jumped across the Rhine to our area of Baden, bringing the simmering pot of discontent to a full boil. Displaced poor, students, and the "federalists" pushing for democracy stirred the pot. Cities all around us exploded into violent demonstrations. Firebrand democrats, like Friedrich Hecker and Gustav Struve, fueled revolutionary fervor among the poor. In Rastatt, Freiburg, and Offenburg, pitched battles at the barricades in the streets resembled those of the French Revolution. Although armed struggle for economic freedom and a German Republic may have seemed necessary to those who felt hopeless, it provoked the aristocracy to rescind our liberal parliament and fight back with Prussian mercenaries.

On Easter Sunday 1849, republican volunteers commandeered cannons and guns from Freiburg's armory. They had no chance against the well-armed Prussian troops, but they fired their weapons nonetheless. Throughout the violent day innocent townspeople died and buildings burned, and by the end of it, the Prussians took back control of the town.

Arrogant Prussian troops then swarmed over the countryside like a conquering army, creating havoc and fear. In Rastatt, they overran the market, overturning tables, scattering carefully crafted wares, and trampling food. They manhandled anyone who stepped in their way. They stole horses and wagons from farmhouses. Even Napoleon's troops had not been as destructive as the Prussians where. Napoleon had wanted our boys. The Prussians wanted our defeat.

One evening in May, as Alex and I settled down to dinner, a cacophony in the street startled us to our feet. We heard the raucous shouting grow steadily louder and closer. Our little bell stuttered with alarm as men outside began battering at our door. The invaders roared out grunts and vulgar oaths. The door reverberated as soldiers slammed their bodies against it. Finally, the old door surrendered to the barrage and, with a raspy screech, tore from its hinges. We heard the muffled sounds of bolts of fabric being tossed and trampled on the floor; the ancient oaken cabinet of small drawers that housed threads, thimbles, pins, and buttons smashed face-first to the floor. The harsh, voices of drunken men shouting in the unmistakable gutturals of Prussian German made the hairs of the back on my neck stand up.

"There is nothing here!" growled an older voice.

"Where's the damn tailor?!" snarled a younger voice. "There must be a cash box here somewhere."

Loud profanity followed the sound of a body hitting the floor. One of the invaders must have fallen to the ground. It sounded as though he was sharply kicked by one of his confederates, provoking guffaws from the observers and more inspired curses from the drunken oaf.

"What the hell are you doing? Don't kick me! I'm not the enemy. Keep looking for that cash box!" he growled.

I tugged Alex to me, and we stood in the center of the room clinging to each other. Alex's arms encircled my waist; my bent torso and arms almost smothered him against my chest. We were standing there when a huge, sodden clout stomped up the stairs and into the room.

"We have nothing!" I screamed at him.

"Where is the tailor? Where does he keep his cash box?" His red-rimmed eyes passed over me, appraising me as if I was nothing more than an old cow.

"I am the tailor." As I said the words, I released Alex from my grip and maneuvered him out of sight behind my voluminous skirts. I straightened, trying to make myself look as large as possible as I held his gaze.

The fool closed his eyes, threw his head back, and laughed with a sound like a rusty metal saw grating against river rock.

I felt Alex creep away behind me, but I stood my ground and did not take my eyes off the vandal who defiled my home.

"You are the tailor? And I am the king of Spain!" he mocked.

"Just leave us alone. If you tore the whole house apart, you would not find a cash box. What you see before you is all we have." My words gave me courage and gave the dumb ox in front of me pause.

He stared at me intently, completely oblivious to Alex's movements. I brazenly stared back, trying to distract him from the missing boy. At that moment, Alex moved deftly in front of me, now holding the heaviest cast iron frying pan we owned.

"You leave my mother alone! We have done nothing against you. We own nothing of any use to you, unless you need needles and pins. You are a chickenhearted coward, threatening a woman, and a traitor to your Prussian commander." Alex held the frying pan poised above his left shoulder, readying his young muscles to swing with every ounce of strength he had.

Our persecutor laughed again, this time more heartily. But then he paused, turned, and clomped back down the stairs without a word.

"There's nothing here, boys. These people are idiots, but poor idiots. Maybe we can convince another tavern keeper to open his doors to us. A few broken windows should do the trick." And they were gone.

After the bedlamites retreated far down the street, Alex and I crept down the stairs.

Together we propped the heavy door up until it leaned crookedly against the doorjamb. I dropped to my knees in the chaos of the shop, smothering my urge to cry into the palms I pressed to my face. Alex approached and faced me. I reached up to wrap my arms around him and held him with a crushing grip. Even the strongest of those degenerates could not have pried my arms from my son.

"Alex, you were so courageous! I am so proud of you. I never would have guessed you had the heart of a lion!" I sputtered.

"Where do you think I learned it?" He smiled impishly, shedding the evening's terror as easily as autumn trees shed their leaves.

With the immediate danger passed, I dissolved into tears. Eventually, I held Alex at arm's length and stared directly into his eyes. For a moment, I saw in those eyes the man he would become. He was a boy poised at the precipice of manhood, tenderly vulnerable, like the defenseless fledgling that will become the eagle.

There would be no peace for us that night in our defiled home. If we had stayed, I would have spent the night waiting for the rowdy troop to return. Alex and I left the front door propped against the door frame and escaped out the back, slinking through the town's quietest streets. The peaks and valleys of the hills carved a flat, dimensionless silhouette against the night sky. We wrapped our coats around us and crept out of town into the black backdrop of mountains. We walked the few miles to the Schultz's farm, abandoning the house exactly as the invaders had left it.

We roused the sleeping family with fists hammering at the door. As calmly as we could, we shared our story of the evening's terror. Clem muttered angrily. Hilda clutched her shawl around her in frightened silence as her children clung to her nightdress.

"I am moving back home with you! It is not safe for you to be alone with this constant unrest raging through the entire countryside." Peter bolted to his feet.

"I am not alone. You should have seen your brave little brother scare them away with the frying pan."

All eyes turned to Alex fidgeting grimly in his seat.

"He was ferocious, a real warrior!" Admiration infused my words.

Peter looked approvingly at his brother. "I'm sure he was very brave. But you were lucky. Things could have ended horribly. Haven't you been reading the gazettes? Those Prussians march in and act as if the whole place was rightfully theirs. They are terrorizing the countryside," Peter wailed.

"Yes, you must be at home to protect your mother," Clem Schultz agreed. "We will figure out how to handle your responsibilities here. Go back home with your mother tomorrow. She needs you now. Anastasia and Alex will stay here with us tonight." Clem settled the matter.

The following day I returned home with Alex and Peter to face the task of assessing our losses and putting the shop back together again. For the first time in many years, I had both of my boys with me again. Like crusaders after a long absence to a foreign country, we learned how to be a true family once more.

With skills he learned from nine years with the Schultz's, Peter transformed Francisca's all-but-abandoned garden into an efficient tiny farm. We returned to market days, displaying my needlework and Peter's produce and basketry. Our unusual variety of goods attracted more curiosity than customers, until one day in autumn.

Peter had stayed home to tend to repairs in our neglected house. A distinguished man with a long, black handlebar mustache and a brocade vest stretched snuggly across his ample belly stopped to investigate Peter's tall backpack baskets. He lingered for quite a while, inspecting every detail. I stood by mutely as he looked. Finally, he removed the ornately carved Meerschaum pipe from between his teeth and spoke.

"I am Konrad Gagel," he said by way of introduction.

"Good day, Herr Gagel. Can I help you?" I answered.

When it was clear I did not recognize his name, he continued without any show of modesty. "I am the most successful basket dealer in the country. I distribute my products more widely than anyone else. Who made these baskets?" His abrupt manner startled me.

"My son, Peter, made them. He trained at Lichtenfels. Perhaps you are acquainted with the well-respected school for basketry located there." I returned his frankness with my own.

He leveled his cool gaze at me. "Ah, no wonder then. You will tell him to meet me here tomorrow," he replied with an air of someone accustomed to immediate compliance.

"Of course, Herr Gagel. I'm sure he will be delighted to meet you. He will see you here tomorrow."

As I walked home with my basket of unsold vegetables, I pondered the significance of this encounter. I didn't know who Konrad Gagel was, but somehow I felt that his interest made our investment in Peter's schooling worth every taler Francisca and I had scraped together.

"Mother, this is wonderful!" It was, refreshing to see Peter so enlivened by the news.

"Do you know him?" I asked.

"Of course! Everyone at the school in Lichtenfels spoke about his successful brokerage as if he invented commerce. Konrad Gagel's company is the largest basket broker in the country. His sales representatives travel with a pattern book of thousands of baskets to show prospective customers. Konrad Gagel buys only the best pieces from hundreds of basket makers and sells them throughout the country. Each basket maker receives a royalty for every basket his company sells." Peter was almost breathless.

"Do you understand what this means?" He gripped my two shoulders with his muscular hands.

I had to admit that I did not.

"It means that I will have a reliable market for my baskets. That market will include the entire country. My baskets will be sold in places I could never go. I will have a steady source of income! Mother, I will be able to marry!"

Just as I had never thought of Peter's future job prospects, his marriage prospects had never occurred to me. Naturally he would want to marry. He was twenty-six years old and entitled to a life and family of his own.

After his work was judged to meet the highest standards, Peter began to supply baskets to Herr Gagel. Each month, he received an order he needed to fill on time, or he would be dropped from Gagel's list of suppliers. I didn't think Peter could be more serious and dedicated than he already was, but I was wrong. I cannot imagine a more industrious worker. He saved every taler he could. His future glowed on the horizon like the promise of a new dawn. As happy as I was for him, however, I could not help wonder what lay beyond the horizon for me.

154

CHAPTER 14

GOING AWAY

1855–1861

Peter, Francisca, Alex, and I sat in the buttery yellow corona of light cast from the gas lantern above the kitchen table. We were together again, blanketed against the frigid New Year's Day weather by the warm, effortless comfort of quiet family intimacy. Francisca never failed to visit during the Christmas season. She would not be leaving on the train today as she had planned. The wedged plow on the train's steam engine could not conquer the superior forces of wind-drifted snow. A forlorn Christmas tree stood in the center of the room, its dried needles dusting the wooden planks. Though the holiday had passed, we did not want to remove it while all of us were still together.

Peter's strong hands bent the willow switches he had bathed in his special "soup," rendering them as pliant as the pea vines that weave their own mysterious basketry against a garden trellis. I mended trousers, restitched frayed buttonholes, and gave new life to old skirts, adding borders and piping to hide their threadbare hems. Francisca, still harboring the spirit of the holiday, tatted lovely star-shaped ornaments like Mama used to make, to add to her new family's Christmas tree next year.

Alex was pacing the floor. Now fifteen, he had finished with his formal schooling, and though his marks in school were at the top of his class, he knew he would never be able to attend the gymnasium. He was a volcano of pent-up intensity, looking for a crack into which his molten energy could flow.

"Won't you please sit down, Alex? You are distracting me from my work." I dropped my mending into my lap and rubbed my stinging eyes. Lately when I raised my eyes from close work, they did not refocus on distant objects for many blurry minutes.

"Your work," he stated bluntly. "I've been thinking, Mama, that I need to find work, too. Peter went to work when he was younger than I am now."

"He's right," Francisca interjected. "He is at the right age to find a craft or go to the mines or factories up north."

"Oh, God forbid that he should go to the mines or factories! Yes, they offer steady work, but it is mind-numbing, soul-deadening work. Alex, what would you like to do? I suspect you've been stewing over this question for quite a while." As it had been with Peter, years had bled into each other like an improperly dyed fabric. And I was taken by surprise realizing that Alex was ready to start on his own path to adulthood.

"Yes, actually, I have. I have been visiting Herr Baumgartner's shop with you since I was a small boy. His son is my best schoolmate. Herr Baumgartner has offered me an apprenticeship."

"But you have never shown an interest in my work," I objected weakly, though I did not have a better idea. I knew I could not offer him the kind of apprenticeship my father had offered me. I did not have standing with the guild, and though it's power had weakened over the years, it was still the surest way to a secure livelihood. Besides, I could hardly call myself a tailor anymore. My business consisted mainly of piecework and occasional dressmaking for the women Herr Baumgartner referred to me.

"No, I suppose I haven't," Peter replied. "But the way I look at it, I must certainly have picked up some tricks of the trade. I've been immersed in tailoring my entire life. It seems like good, worthy work, and I can practice my trade wherever I go. It is as portable as a set of good shears, a measuring tape, and a basket of thread. It could be the passport to my future."

Peter, Francisca, and I simultaneously lifted our eyes and exchanged stupefied looks. Alex had a way of shocking us with unexpected revelations. Though my mouth hung wordlessly agape, Peter picked up the thread of the conversation.

"Alex, have you thought this through? Are you sure you could stick to this path?" Peter asked seriously.

"I'll never know until I try, will I?" replied Alex. His restless nature stood in sharp contrast to Peter's gravity. His active mind had always bounced in one direction and then another, like a child's ball bounces off the pavement.

"I will pay him a visit next week, and, if Herr Baumgartner is willing to take you on, we will make the arrangements. Of course, you will continue to live at home. There is no need for him to provide you with room and board. He would no doubt happily take advantage of saving the cost of housing and feeding you. I think I can see how this might be appealing to Herr Baumgartner." I felt my enthusiasm grow as I spoke my thoughts out loud. "He knows you, so he can clearly see you would not cause him trouble, as an unknown apprentice might. And I'm sure he recognizes how quickly you learn."

Over the next several weeks, I settled the arrangements with Herr Baumgartner. Our relationship, though it could not be called a real friendship, had warmed in the years since I'd first visited his shop in a defensive huff. He still pointed a few women clients in my direction, helping to keep my dressmaking business alive, if barely. He had become a well-respected fixture in the community. I was happy that Alex had an honorable man to teach him the trade and that he would not have to face his transition into manhood in the overheated cauldron of social unrest that had prevailed over the past several years.

The boiling pot of upheaval, violence, burning barricades, and Prussian soldiers rampaging through our streets had finally subsided to a simmer. But the poverty and suffering of the Hunger Years had not. Those years when rains would not fall were followed by years when they would not stop. Meager crops rotted in the fields. Each year more destitute people begged in the streets and markets or went from door to door, sadly pulling dirty children behind them. Every week at Sunday Mass, the priest encouraged us to donate to the Church's fund for feeding the poor. After all, hadn't Jesus told us that to care for the least of these was to care for Him? We knew our Christian duty, but many of us had no more to give. Peter, always the sincerely devout believer, surreptitiously pilfered money from my hidden kaffee pot to help the poor. The community was feeding, clothing, and caring for hundreds of paupers. But the patience of most people was wearing thin.

Early in 1855, as tattered remains of gray, ragged snowbanks lined the streets, the burghers of the town met with the pastors of the Church to enact a plan. Church coffers and municipal rainy-day funds had run dry. Even the grand duchy contributed to the plan concocted by town leaders. If the town could not afford to continue supporting the poorest among us, it might be more cost-effective to give them an opportunity to make lives for themselves in America. After all, so many of our people had already voluntarily chosen this path and emigrated to the supposed "land of opportunity." This hard reasoning was fiscally sound perhaps, but the human cost was staggering.

On a gray winter day, as a biting wind swirled around us, we towns-people gathered at St. Michael's to witness the proceedings. Three hundred souls—men, women, and weary, hollow-eyed children—shivered on the church steps. They wore new clothes the townspeople had provided them and clutched old burlap sacks for luggage. Each family had been given 150 gulden each. Tears flowed as fifty-seven families realized they would never see their beautiful green valley again. Five gendarmes marched them out of town toward the Rhine and on to Strasburg. A few days later, they departed on two steamships bound for New Orleans. They would have to make their destiny in a foreign land, where they did not speak the language and knew no one except each other. I could not help wondering what Father would have thought. My heart twisted inside my chest, knowing that "there but for the grace of God go I."

This forced deportation of our poor was a far cry from the voluntary exile the previous year, when Father Ambros Oschwald and 113 of his followers had emigrated to the wilderness of eastern Wisconsin. I could understand why his followers willingly undertook the difficult migration. After all, more than three thousand of his followers believed they had been miraculously healed by Oschwald. He was a charismatic leader who practiced what he preached, often spending whatever money he had helping the poor and espousing the Gospel's most important message, to love one's neighbor. Oschwald believed he had a special, direct relationship with God and could interpret dreams, including his own. One of his dreams was to establish a utopian community, a "New Jerusalem" that would pursue God's work communally.

Trouble had been brewing for Oschwald for several years. Oschwald's followers were devoted to him. The bishops were alarmed by accounts of his seemingly miraculous healing powers and considered them heretical.

They thought his mesmerizing influence over his followers threatened the power of the Church. In an effort to marginalize him, the bishops had exiled Oschwald to a series of remote villages. One of them was Herrenweis, a tiny hamlet a few miles above our town. It was remote and primitive in comparison to Gruntal. We considered it the "Siberia" of our corner of the world. The bishop continued to hound Oschwald into silence until he officially gave up his holy orders and asked permission to emigrate.

Peter had been curious about the priest for years. He had made several treks to the hinterland to visit the dark, little Herrenweis church. Oschwald's teachings resonated with Peter's own ardent beliefs. Peter begged me for permission to leave with the pioneers. He was thirty-one, strong, with highly valuable farming and craft skills—exactly the kind of skills the emigrants would need to carve a utopia out of the wilderness. Several of his friends, people he had known from the church in Herrenweis, followed Oschwald to Le Havre where their adventure began.

Even though I knew how ardently he longed to join the pioneers, I spoke up to oppose the plan. In the end, as much as he wanted to, Peter could not abandon me. Though he did not complain, I could see his longing for the path not taken when he read the gazette articles describing the departure of Oschwald and his band of loyal followers. He would not abandon me, a sixty-one-year-old seamstress with failing eyesight, to fend for myself. The matter was put to rest, and for several years, we carried on as before.

* * *

Carolina came as a blessing. At thirty-four, she might have been considered a spinster when Peter discovered her. Not surprisingly, they met at church. The flame that glowed between them ignited rapidly, and after a courtship of only six months, they married. She came from a very large family and was more than happy to move to our quiet, little house. Peter's bed was the first she had shared with only one other person, unlike the childhood bed she had shared with two sisters. Carolina had a placid demeanor. Almost as tall as Peter, with uncontrollable blond curls, a soft voice, and a ready smile, she stole my heart as surely as she had Peter's. I hadn't realized how sorely I had missed the company of another woman in my home.

In a few years, there was more than just one reason for Peter to stay in Gruntal. Christmas morning 1861 was magical. That autumn had been mild, and even in late November some of the streams still held unfrozen water dancing free. A sudden cold snap reminded us winter wasn't going to pass us by. Schultz's old wagon clattered across the cobblestones, with Peter perched on the high seat. The arms of Peter's wife, Carolina, encircled one-year old Franz, who fidgeted on her lap. I sat bundled up next to them. My mind drifted all the way back to my own childhood, when Father had driven the wagon up to the woodlot to search for the perfect tree. The sudden iciness of the day shocked us out of our late autumn complacency. Our reward for braving the cold was a beautiful pastel sunrise tinting the mist coming off the freezing water a delicate, dusty rose. Every surface was covered with crystalline frosting.

Picking the perfect Tannenbaum was a ritual Peter loved as much as Father had. Little Franz tottered around, barely able to bend his knees in his heavy, wool pants. His little arms protruded from his torso like the stick arms of a snowman.

Decorating the tree with Franz's "help" was troublesome. After two days of prying low-hanging ornaments from Franz's greedy fists, we surrendered and decorated only the upper branches. Peter placed the precious gold star Gilly had found in the Christmas market so long ago on the topmost branch. Alex arranged Mama's tatted stars, and Carolina lit the candles. The strains of our Stille Nacht song drifted through the room, probing every corner for memories of past Christmases.

On the first day of 1862, the shop bells trilled as Francisca and Ignaz entered the shop, stomping the newly fallen snow from their shoes. Since the Ignaz's children and grandchildren were grown, with family traditions of their own, Francisca and Ignaz had been taking the train to Gruntal to help us celebrate our family's New Year traditions.

After our clock chimed twelve times, announcing the New Year, I tippled out drams of the brandy Francisca had brought. I laid limp chunks of pickled herring and crackers on each plate. We lifted our glasses and, as loudly as we could, yelled, "Prost!"

After the toast, we all huddled around a candle in the center of the table, each of us holding a spoon filled with a dab of soft lead. We took turns melting our lead pellet over the candle and dropping it into a bowl of water. Our lead pellets contorted into odd forms as they cooled. We peered into the bowl, trying to divine the shape of our future from the shape of the cooled lead.

"Look, mine is the shape of a swaddled baby!" Carolina laughed.

"I love that prediction. I'm hoping for many more babies." Peter winked at Carolina, making her cheeks flush with pleasure. "Maybe our next baby will be a girl. Can you tell that from the lead?" Peter was as happy as I had ever seen him. He was a stern but affectionate father and a considerate, tender husband. I marveled at this wonderful man, lovingly teasing his wife.

Alex took his turn last.

"It looks like a boot!" I offered after his drop of molten lead wiggled into a vaguely angled shape.

"Well, isn't that interesting!" he replied. "I was hoping to begin my wander years next spring. A boot is the perfect omen."

Once again, Alex took us all by surprise with his unexpected announcement.

"Remember the stories Father used to tell about his wander years?" said Francisca, her face ruddy and eyes drooping slightly from the several rounds of good cheer we'd shared.

"Yes, of course! I remember how dreamy he became, talking about the splendors of Vienna and his beloved schneidermeister, Herr Buchlieber," I said. "His books are still right there on our shelves. Of course, their edges are a bit furred from being read so often. Good old Herr Buchlieber! Prost!" I called.

"Vienna," Alex said. "That sounds perfect."

"The world isn't the same as it was then, dear. The guild system is a dim shadow of what it used to be in your grosspapa's time," I opined.

"That's true, but the tradition hasn't died. Herr Baumgartner will get me a *wanderbuch* and a letter of introduction to present at the guild halls of cities I visit. I can follow in my grandfather's footsteps and see where they take me. I might even find a bride, like he did." Alex beamed. The wanderlust was upon him. Though I worried for his safety, I knew I had to let him go. He would be twenty-three years old soon and fully capable of making his way in the world. It was time for him to satisfy his restless, adventurous nature.

CINDY MAYNARD

"Besides," put in the usually silent Ignaz, "he has the three primary qualifications of a journeyman. He is single, childless, and without debt. In our neighborhood, near the gymnasium in Offenburg, we often see journeymen of various trades wandering the streets. They come from many places and are an interesting addition to the town."

"Let's find Father's old costume!" Francisca enthused and promptly flew down the stairs to search the shop.

After a few minutes, Francisca reappeared with a carefully wrapped package. "Here it is! The red tie, the vest, and the jacket with bright silver buttons. It looks like they could use some polishing." She giggled like a schoolgirl.

"Well, it looks like you have your family's approval," I said, feeling rather helpless to stem the tide of rising enthusiasm.

Each of us in turn had managed to find a happy portent in the shapes of our lead balls. Surely, it would be a good year. We talked and laughed until the wee hours, our feet pointed toward the warmth of the fireplace as we nursed our brandy.

It was early the next spring—when the buds of the plum trees, unable to wait for the tardy leaves to catch up, burst into bloom—that Francisca, Peter, his little family, and I accompanied Alex to the edge of town. Herr Baumgartner and his apprentices traipsed noisily through the streets. The young men insisted we stop at the last tavern on the road out of town. There they bought Alex a stein of beer and poured it into Alex's upturned hat. Then, clapping and backslapping, they cheered and shouted as Alex attempted to drink the beer from his hat. At the town signpost, the rest of us stopped as Alex trudged on alone. He never looked back. The ancient journeyman custom forbade him to do so, as it would bring three years of bad luck.

For the next three years, Alex would own nothing but his meager belongings and the tools of his trade carried in his simple knapsack. He would travel only on foot or on the back of a farmer's wagon. He would seek lodgings from strangers or at the journeyman hostels that still existed in the larger cities. His mission was to travel, see the country, study with the best mentors he could find, perfect his craft, and learn to be his own man.

The high-spirited young apprentices returned to the tavern, while Peter,

Franz, and his pregnant wife, Carolina, returned home. Francisca and I lingered on the road, watching Alex disappear into the hills. When we finally pried our eyes from Alex's disappearing figure and looked at each other, we both had tears in our eyes.

"Our baby," I said. "Our 'foundling.'"

As we turned to go, Francisca took my hand, and we slowly walked home.

CHAPTER 15

ALONE

1863–1867

In autumn, I received a priceless gift—better than the nuts, fruits, and sweets hidden in our shoes when we were children—a letter from Alex. It had been more than a year since we had watched Alex disappear into the hills. My hands shook as I opened the letter:

> June 1863
>
> Dear Mama, Tante Mausi, and Peter,
>
> I have tramped over four hundred miles since I left Gruntal last spring. I was grateful for the money my friends stuffed into my pockets as I left home. I needed nearly every penny of it to buy new boots. I am writing to you from Vienna. It is everything I thought it would be, such a beautiful city I can't begin to describe it. Sadly, Herr Buchlieber is long dead, and no one remembers a journeyman named Anton Burkart. The tailor shop where he worked has been replaced by a little store selling factory-made shirts and trousers. But I found a real tailor and applied there to work as journeyman. Two other journeymen sat atop the oak table when I arrived. The master tailor, Herr Tuchmann, is a jovial man who welcomed me aboard. I know I will be happy here, at least for a while.
>
> My first year, I trekked from Gruntal to Augsburg, through the familiar landscape of the Black Forest and then

over the Swabian Alps. They are pretty but no match for our Schartzwald. I could hardly comprehend the bizarre dialect spoken by the people of Swabia. From Augsburg, I decided to avoid climbing more mountains and followed the Danube to Regensburg.

I worked the winter in Regensburg. I found a busy tailor shop to employ me, and for three months, the other apprentices, journeymen, and I formed a cordial fraternity. It was fascinating to watch stonemasons, carvers, and bricklayers swarm fearlessly over the high scaffolding surrounding the towers of the old Gothic cathedral. The rest of the cathedral had been completed two centuries ago. No one seemed to know why it took over four hundred years to finish the towers. On my way out of town, I walked in the footsteps of the crusaders over the old stone bridge that spanned the Danube. By spring, my feet were fully recovered, and they itched for the byways again.

I might have enjoyed spending some time in Munich, but Franz, a fellow journeyman I met in Regensberg, persuaded me to set out with him directly to Vienna. It was nice to have a traveling companion for a while.

The wandering life suits me. Every day there are new people to meet. If I want a change of scenery, I know that my commitment to my master tailor will be over in three months, and I will be free to walk on. My thoughts are my companions. My eyes are my windows to the world, and the view is glorious. There certainly have been hardships, like sleeping on the ground, only to wake in the morning surrounded by cow droppings and the square pink noses of cows puffing low over my face. There have been days of misery, slogging down muddy paths, soaked to the skin by relentless rain. I have gotten lost once or twice but soon found my way again.

The people I have met along the way all speak German of one sort or another. My journeyman's costume elicits curiosity. Most folks are happy to help me. Once I was accosted by a gang of youths who thought my meager pack must hold riches. But a few well-aimed blows from my walking staff put an end to that. After the discomforts of the road have passed, their memory recedes quickly, and the open road beckons me forward.

I think Vienna will hold my interest for quite some time. On my return journey, I might like to see Munich or Salzburg, or maybe both.

I keep you in my prayers, as I hope you are keeping me in yours.

Your loving son,

Alex

That was the last I heard from him until he reappeared one day in 1865. Peter's oldest child, Franz, now five years old, came clamoring up the stairs forgetting to close the door. The noisy autumn wind blew a scrim of fallen leaves behind him into the shop's open door.

"Oma, Oma, Alex is home! Come now!" he shrieked before charging back out the still-open door.

I surprised myself with how quickly my sixty-nine-year-old legs could carry me as I hustled to the edge of town where we had bid Alex goodbye three years earlier. A small crowd gathered around the town signpost. Alex's young friends from Herr Baumgartner's shop, Herr Baumgartner, and some newcomers milled around. Alex stood on the other side waiting for me to appear. As soon as I was within a stone's throw, he climbed up the signpost, went over the top, and officially reentered Gruntal. Herr Baumgartner ceremoniously inspected his wanderbuch, officially declaring that he had successfully completed his journey. Shouts and applause greeted Alex as the welcoming swarm swept into the tavern. My wandering son embraced me against his strapping frame, picked me up, and swung me around as he would a child. His shoulders were broader, his face a little more weather-beaten. But he was glowing with the fullness of young manhood. After sharing a stein with the well-wishers, I returned home to make a special homecoming dinner.

Alex's cheeks were ruddy and his eyes bleary with drink when he finally joined us. He exuded the aura of a conquering hero. Peter was solemn. He and Carolina had produced two children in the three footloose years Alex had traveled the country and beyond. Peter, anchored as he was by his young family, had not ventured farther than the Schultz's farm, the market, and the forest trails.

"Hello, brother!" Alex jovially slapped Peter's back. "I see you've kept yourself busy here with Carolina." Alex laughed raucously.

"Please, Alex, don't be coarse," Peter grumbled.

Alex's face fell. None of us expected Peter's gruff manner, not even Peter. Alex's triumphal return seemed to trigger a smoldering resentment. The long-awaited homecoming pivoted abruptly from joyous to awkward.

Alex picked up his knapsack and announced, "I can see you are crowded here in the house and won't have room for me with Peter's family living here. I'm sure Herr Baumgartner would like to hear more about my wanderings." And he marched out the door.

I was crestfallen. I slumped in a chair at the table laden with sauerbraten, potatoes, and beans, Alex's favorite meal. We hadn't heard one word about his adventures. We hadn't even had a real conversation.

Peter quietly stood behind my chair and put a hand on my shoulder. "I'm sorry, Mama. I should have given my brother a more enthusiastic welcome. I don't know what came over me. I may not be as adventurous as he, but ever since Father Oschwald left with his band of pioneers, I have been haunted by the idea of joining his holy mission in the wilds of the new world," he confessed. "I wonder when I will get my turn at adventure."

The following week, I at last had the pleasure of one full day with Alex, just the two of us. Peter was out tending the strong, pliable willows he grew especially for his coal-carrying baskets, and Carolina had taken the children to see her mother for the day, so the house was quiet. Alex and I worked together in the shop, he sitting cross-legged on the tailoring table, as all tailors did, and I in my soft chair embroidering pillowcases for a customer. He filled my ears with the grandeur of Vienna, the pleasure of traveling, the camaraderie of friends, and how his journey years had changed him. He was a man now, reveling in his independence, confident of his ability to adapt to nearly every situation and make his way in the world.

"I almost forgot." He jumped off the table with the grace and agility of a cat and began digging in his knapsack. "I've carried this over three hundred miles, since I spent my winter in Regensburg, to give to you. It is a German translation of a very popular English book." He beamed as he presented me with a thick book, its leather cover battered but intact.

"*A Tale of Two Cities.*" I read the book cover. "I have heard of this author, Charles Dickens. Thank you so much, Alex. You carried this book all that way for me? How thoughtful of you!"

"You will love this book! I was able to find a rare German translation. I know how you crave new books." He bowed, one hand crossed over his chest, the other holding the book out to me on his open palm, like a courtier at a queen's throne.

I wrapped my arms around his shoulders. "I missed you so much. I'm glad you are finally home." Though I tried to control my emotions, a happy tear squeezed out between my lids.

"Yes, well, I won't be staying for long." He lowered his voice. "There is no work for me in this town," he grumbled.

Once again, Alex ambushed me with his abrupt pronouncements. There was nothing I could say or do to stop him. He was a grown man. My wish to keep him close to home carried little weight.

"But Alex, you just got here! Where will you go?" I whined.

"I have seen much of our old world, and now I want to see the new world."

"The new world? Do you mean America? Are you emigrating?" My eyebrows shot up to my hairline. My mouth formed a perfect "O."

"No Mama, I don't want to settle down yet. I want to see the world. The French Foreign Legion will take nearly any able-bodied man who signs on, and they go anywhere they are asked." His devil-may-care attitude was simply stunning! And I was duly stunned.

"That sounds preposterous! The French Foreign Legion? Do you want to be a soldier now?"

"No, not a solder, a tailor. I have a portable trade. It can take me wherever I want to go. And the legion will pay my passage to America."

I couldn't believe my ears, but Alex was completely serious. True to his word, later that summer, Alex crossed the Rhine to Strasburg and enlisted in the French Foreign Legion. He disappeared as abruptly as he'd appeared only a few months before.

Many months passed before I received any letter. It was short and terse, nothing like the effusive missive I'd received from Vienna. I wondered if he was sorry for his decision. In the clipped words of a military man, he curtly informed me that he had been assigned to join Maximillian's forces in Mexico. I had read about Maximillian. His mission was so improbable it was almost incomprehensible. In an attempt to gain a foothold in the Americas, France had invaded Mexico a few years ago, even though Mexico had its own government, a liberal administration headed by Benito Juarez. Napoleon III had invited Maximillian to establish a monarchy for him and force Juarez out of power. After Maximillian landed in Mexico, he must have begun having delusions of grandeur. In 1864, Maximillian declared himself emperor of Mexico. The whole situation made no sense to me.

What I read in the gazettes about the rash operation was not comforting. Conditions were primitive; disease was rampant. The legionnaires were a motley crew of ne'er-do-wells, ruffians, and criminals. They could not have been edifying company for my Alex.

In his letter, Alex assured me he would be fine, and I was not to worry. He was simply a tailor, following the troops, mending uniforms. Although he carried a weapon, so far, he said, he had not had to use it. The thought of Alex carrying weapons unsettled me, and not having to use them gave me little reassurance.

I knew very little of this wild, foreign land. I read as much as I could, but our local gazettes filled their pages with minute details of local events and devoted only a little space to events outside our borders. Never in my wildest imagination did I ever think I would need to forage the newsstands in the market for information about developments in Mexico.

My resolve to do as Alex suggested and not worry dissolved in late June 1867 when the *Freiburg Gazette* headlines shouted, "Maximillian Executed in Mexico." There is no feeling worse than that of a mother who is helpless to save her child. I didn't sleep that night worrying about what would happen to my brave, restless son.

By the end of the summer, however he was back in Gruntal.

When he opened the door and marched up the stairs, I did not recognize him. I had a moment of panic thinking he was one of the soldiers who'd invaded our home and threatened us decades ago. The uniform did not suit him—baggy red pants, tight-fitting navy blue jacket, and a ridiculous straw hat with a wide circular brim that circumnavigated his entire head. And he sported a wide, bushy mustache.

"Jesus, Mary, and Joseph!" I almost screamed.

"Mama, it's me, Alex." He laughed in an untroubled voice.

Yes, it was my Alex, as strong and rugged as ever. "You're back! They didn't kill you!"

"No, Mama, they decided to get rid of us, packed us up, and sent us home." He seemed less lighthearted than the fearless young man who'd left to join the legionnaires. He was sobered but was not ruined by war as the soldiers returning to Gruntal from Napoleon's ill-fated war in Russia had been.

"For some unknown reason, the Mexicans wanted to govern themselves without our help." A wry smile crept across his face.

"Oh, dear Lord. You're safe, you're safe. Now, surely, you will settle down. You must have seen enough of the world by now."

"No, Mama. I am still obliged to finish my term of service with the legion. They are sending me away again."

I did not protest, though I would have shackled him to the table if I thought it would prevent him from leaving. I knew there was no point. My exclamations and wailings would only make him feel worse. I wanted only to comfort him. "Where will they send you now?" I choked out the words.

"I am going to the deserts of Algeria to fight the wild tribes. But remember, Mama, I am just a tailor. My job is to mend, not to destroy. I have seen uniforms torn to bits. I have seen the men who wore those uniforms lacerated to shreds. The greatest dangers I have faced have come from disease and the brutal climate, not from enemy swords. Please, do not worry for me." He seemed genuinely concerned for my sorrow.

"That's impossible," I replied bluntly.

"Well then, transform your worries into prayers for me. There is nothing more you can do for me." He was resigned to face whatever came next with bravery and fortitude.

In return, I promised to pray as I had never done before, and so I did. Then my Alex disappeared from my life once again.

Carolina and Peter now had three little ones, Franz, Mary, and baby Ellen. Our small house was so crowded I began to sleep in the shop downstairs. It was increasingly difficult for me, at age seventy-on, to climb the stairs. But giving Peter and his family as much room as they needed was a necessary adjustment. Ever since Alex had come home from his journey years, Carolina and Peter spent more and more time at church, often meeting with other parents of young families. During the summer, Peter became increasingly restive and preoccupied. He avoided looking at me directly, as if he was keeping a secret he didn't want me to know.

Finally, on a balmy evening in late June, the truth came out. Peter and Carolina confronted me. For months, they had been making plans to immigrate to Wisconsin to join Father Oschwald's community in St. Nazianz. Peter confided that he had been corresponding with a friend who'd moved with the original band of 113 settlers. The intrepid pioneers had managed, despite many hardships, to carve a thriving little town from the wilderness. He had assured Peter that, though Wisconsin did not have a climate suitable for growing wine grapes, a man with his extensive farming and basket making experience would be welcomed.

Peter explained the route they would take on the long journey to Wisconsin—north along the Rhine to Rotterdam and then across the English Channel, around the southern coast of England to Liverpool, where they would board the steam ship *Tarifa* to New York. From there, smaller boats would take them on a circuitous route, first to Albany, New York, and then on steamboat via the Erie Canal to Buffalo and then across Lake Erie to Cleveland, Detroit, and Milwaukee. In Milwaukee, Peter's friend would shepherd them to St. Nazianz. They would be following the route taken by the original settlers thirteen years ago. The journey, he patiently explained, would be mostly by water and would take three months. I had sorely misunderstood Peter's resolve to follow Oschwald.

The plan was to leave before an ocean passage became too treacherous. Peter, Carolina, and my three grandbabies planned to embark on November 16, 1867. Traveling halfway across the world with a wife, a seven-year-old son, a four-year-old daughter, and another daughter not yet one-year-old, was beyond my ability to imagine. Peter had been my rock, an island of stability in uncertain times. I had always felt safe and secure in his strong hands. I'd never expected my serious, reliable son to desert me in my old age.

"But, Mama," he argued. "I am forty-four years old, and Carolina is forty-one. This is our last chance to fulfill our dreams. We love you, but we must do this for our children. We are giving them a future full of unimagined possibilities. We will live among like-minded believers, all working for the glory of God. I've never made a secret of wanting to share in Father Oschwald's vision. Carolina and I have been dreaming of this for a long time."

I could not form words to answer. All I could do was cry. I made no pretense of being strong or stoic. I had no words of support or wise counsel. My heart was broken. Peter's mind was made up. He had spent many months planning and would not be turned away from his purpose.

That Christmas, I was alone—no sons, no grandchildren, no sister. I was an abandoned old lady, with failing eyesight and fingers painfully bent with arthritis, barely able to support myself. I allowed myself to sink beneath the waves of darkness that submerged all my hope. I went to bed and turned my face to the wall.

CHAPTER 16

DARKNESS TO LIGHT

1868–1872

On January 1, 1868, Francisca thrust open the front door, setting the bell ringing. Her New Year visit had become our tradition. She swept up the stairs clutching bottles of milk that had curdled on my doorstep.

The parlor was dark and cold. Small drifts of fine snow edged the windowsills. Drifts of dust balls hugged the corners of the room. Though I had barely eaten in weeks, the dishes I had used were piled in disorderly stacks in the sink. I didn't move when I heard her enter the house. My body and soul were frozen into a shriveled husk of a person curled in bed, face to the wall.

"Oh, dear God!" Francisca shrieked in alarm. "Ignaz, please stoke the wood stove, start a fire in the hearth, and for heaven's sake light the gas lamp!"

If I had been fully conscious, it would have been surprising to hear her order her mild-mannered husband around. I could hear Ignaz bustling around the parlor.

She turned her attention back to me. "Anastasia! Anastasia! What's wrong with you? Are you ill? Do I need to call the doctor?" When she got no response, she grabbed my shoulder, forcefully rolled me onto my back, and confronted me face-to-face.

I stared at her. My mind comprehended what was happening, but I could not command my voice to speak. I felt as if I were totally detached from my body, gazing down on the unfolding drama from a corner of the ceiling.

"Anastasia! Answer me!" she cried, but she did not wait for an answer. She swept out of the room and put a pot of water to boil on the woodstove.

I retreated back into my internal landscape of despair.

When Francisca returned, she and Ignaz firmly forced my body into a sitting position. Supporting the back of my head with her steady hand, she coaxed hot tea between my lips. I saw her and Ignaz exchange glances. Over the next hour, they warmed my body and the house. Reviving my will to speak took longer.

"Anastasia, you know I have seen this behavior before. Remember when Gilly died?" Her low, almost whispered voice sent a jolt rippling through my body as I remembered my beloved brother. "I was very young, only six, but I remember how Mama retreated into her sorrow."

Finally I spoke. "You were there to keep her alive, Mausi. If it hadn't been for you, she would never have returned to us. She brought herself out of the gloom for you, Francisca. But I have no one to left live for." I spoke in a papery whisper.

She did not contradict me. "I will stay with you as long as I must. I will not allow you to do this. It's not fair. I have Ignaz's family, but you are my only real family, and I will not let you do this. It's not fair to me!" Her words expressed more love than any words of endearment ever could.

"I will try."

And so I did. Returning from profound disassociation was painful and difficult. But I did try to stay in the present moment as best I could.

For six months, Francisca remained with me. She resumed her domestic routines as though she had never left. It was comforting to me, and over time, I began to feel grounded once more in the world of the living.

Before she left for her own home, she insisted on accompanying me to the Schultz's for Sunday dinner. Clem Schultz was a patriarch now. His children had produced an abundance of grandchildren. The oldest son, whom Peter had helped train, was now managing the various farming operations. The daughters had married well, to railroad managers and bankers, and lived nearby, free from economic worry.

"Dear Anastasia," Herr Schultz greeted me warmly. "How have you been faring? Are you still working as a tailor? I heard Peter moved to

America. And what part of the wide world has Alex gotten himself to? Last I heard, he had run off and joined the French Foreign Legion."

Clem's wife, Hilda, ushered us into the house and settled us at a table piled high with an abundant dinner.

"We are so glad to share this meal with you," Francisca broke in. "You and Anastasia can bring each other up to date with your family's lives. But first I would like to ask you a special favor."

"Of course, I would be happy to do whatever I can do for you."

"Anastasia has been living alone for quite a while. Would you be so kind as to stop by and check in on her from time to time? Maybe Hilda would enjoy market day with Anastasia, or one of your older grandchildren could help her with some of the more difficult maintenance jobs around the house. Anastasia can no longer manage all that by herself. She has been spending too much time alone, I fear." She made these favors sound as common as spring rain. She expressed no hint of embarrassment or shame. I, on the other hand, felt very ashamed, an old lady living alone. I had taken care of my family my whole life and was now unable to care even for myself.

Herr Schultz's banter dried up and his tone became solicitous. "Yes, of course. I understand. We will make sure Anastasia is well looked after. It will be our pleasure. Your family has been almost as dear to us as our own. If things had gone differently in Napoleon's war …" His voice trailed off. "Well, things might have been very different."

"Thank you," Francisca said.

At that, we settled down to enjoy Sunday dinner. As the conversation swirled around me, a little more life creep back into my soul.

Before Francisca left to return to her husband, we had a similar encounter with Herr Baumgartner. He began to ask about Alex's whereabouts but stopped when he understood the seriousness of Francisca's request for help for me.

After that meeting, Herr Baumgartner made sure one of his apprentices delivered small sewing jobs to me on a weekly basis. He paid me generously for my work. I began to feel I could once again support myself. I received occasional gifts from my friends and a steady stream of work from Herr Baumgartner, but this support bolstered my self-respect more than I could have imagined. To me, it meant that I was valued by them. I no longer felt so alone. A lifetime of shared experiences tethered me to my friends.

By the time Alex returned at Christmas of 1869, I was once again functioning almost normally, though not with my previous vigor. He whisked in to the house with dramatic flair. But this time, he was wearing civilian clothes.

He swept me up in his arms and then held me back at arm's length and looked at me closely. "Mama, you are smaller. I could pick you up with one hand." He examined me with a combination of concern and fascination.

"Alex, my dear Alex. You're home. I have had such little news from you," I said more in wonder than to scold.

"Yes, Mama, I know. I'm sorry. We will have many hours before the fire this season for me to describe the howling tribes of Berbers, the blinding desert sandstorms, and all my adventures." He stopped to consider. "Well, almost all my adventures." He smiled and winked at me.

I laughed out loud, my first real laugh since I'd returned from the precipice of despair. I threw my arms around him, and tears of joy seeped from my eyes. This must be why I had not been allowed to leave this world yet. I still had joy to experience.

This year, I did not run through the snow with my little brother, throw snowballs at my sister, or watch a grandson nearly paralyzed by his bulky winter clothes. It was only Alex and me on the hunt for the perfect tree. He bundled me securely in layers of wool and sat me beside him on the old wagon. I watched as he felled the best tree. We worked side by side adorning the tree, each bauble or tatted star holding a memory. I decorated the lowest branches unevenly, as a child would. I sat in my soft chair, no longer in the shop, but installed like a throne next to the fireplace and sipped schnapps as Alex placed the glass star with its chipped gold paint in its place of honor at the top of the tree.

That winter, we talked for hours. Alex had grown into a gregarious man of the world, brimming with exciting stories full of barely believable characters. He attracted friends like spilled sugar attracts ants. Soon, he began to attract young women too. He was thirty years old. He was a highly skilled master tailor, handsome, and delightfully companionable. He went out with friends most evenings, often coming home late, singing happily.

Alex took charge of the shop. I watched as he deposited yellowed paper patterns for long out-of-date clothing styles, useless scraps of fabric, moth-chewed bolts of wool, and water-damaged silk into a pile in the middle of the shop floor. He cleaned windows and reorganized shelves. So much dust flew in the air that he had to prop the front door open. I had not realized how sadly the shop had been neglected. He settled himself on the old oak table and went to work on my mending. Before long, our little bell rediscovered its voice and sang happily as new customers found their way to our shop. I greeted the customers as I had since I was sixteen. Father would have been proud of Alex's success in bringing his business back to life.

Alex attracted friends like sunflowers attracted bees. He started joining the Friday evening schafkopf players who gathered above Herr Seifreid's barbershop. I could imagine knuckles rapping on the kitchen table as guffaws and groans rang out among the players. Herbert Seifried, an old schoolmate of Alex's, lived at home with his unmarried brothers and sister and tended the shop. Soon, Alex was spending quite a bit of time at the barbershop. His hair and mustache were groomed to perfection.

After a while, his demeanor changed. While he was still happy, he seemed less carefree. I began to wonder if something had happened to change his mood.

When spring arrived in 1870, Alex put an end to my speculations.

"Mama, there is someone I want you to meet."

I knew at once he had met a special girl. I could see it in his eyes. I could feel the energy of love emanating from him like steam from a train's smokestack.

"You've met a young lady, haven't you?" I was no stranger to the tidal pull of young love. "Tell me about her. How did you meet her?"

"Her name was Rosina Seifried," he said. "You will like her. She is Herbert Seifried's sister. She is lovely, rather quiet and shy, but once you get to know her, she is charming." His face lit up just talking about her.

Ah, so that explains the recent improvement in his grooming, I thought.

"Please invite her for Sunday dinner. What is her favorite meal? She will be welcome in my house." If Alex loved her, that was enough for me to love her too.

Rosina was a lovely, twenty-four-year-old young lady. Her hair shone as though she had brushed it with polish. She was slightly built and slim waisted. I could see why Alex was smitten with her. It was clear that he loved her in the unequivocal way that a man of the world, who has seen and experienced so much, knows that this woman is the one he was meant for.

"Rosina, my dear girl, I am so happy to meet you. I have missed another woman to share my home with. I'm sure we will become great friends."

She beamed and squeezed Alex's hand just a little harder.

In May 1870, they were married in the same church where I had sung in the choir loft with Rupert Schultz and on whose steps Francisca and I had risked losing Alex in a wild attempt to give him legitimacy. The young couple did not waste time. Exactly nine months after the wedding, Rosina gave birth to their baby girl.

Little Mary was born into a new world. Though our streets wound up and around the surrounding hills as they always had, though the bakery still oozed mouthwatering smells at dawn, and though the market was as noisy and bustling as ever, much had changed for Gruntal and all of Germany.

Since the Enlightenment had first stirred change, ideals of freedom and equality had taken hold. In my lifetime, through wars, riots, famine, and disruption, they had grown and matured. In 1871 Otto von Bismarck declared a new Reich, based on democratic principles. The new Reich united all the German states into one country. Though we were still from the region of Baden, we could now also proudly call ourselves "Germans." Little Mary's world would be governed by a Reichstag parliament; peasants would no longer be bonded to lords of the manor; people could make lives for themselves unfettered by guild laws. Mary would enjoy a freedom unknown in Father's time or in mine.

CHRISTMAS 1872

CLOSING MY BOOK OF DAYS

This Christmas, I stayed home from the hunt for the best Tannenbaum in the forest. I watched little Mary practice walking. She and I laughed together when she lost her balance and she landed with a thump on her well-padded bottom. I tottered a bit myself now, but I was determined to continue working at my craft as long as I could, though my poor eyesight and hands nearly crippled by arthritis prevented me from making perfect stitches as I had in the past. I took great pride in knowing that I had kept the door over the tailor shop ringing long enough for my son to revive his grandfather's business. I was the link from one generation to the next.

I rose from my soft chair and wobbled to my bedroom. I bent down to the ground, reaching under my bed. Mary crawled next to me. "Oma, Oma," she chortled. I pulled out the old Kasperle puppet, the one Gilly had gotten for Christmas so many years ago. Though she was too young for it, I brought it back to the parlor and gave it to Mary. I sat back and enjoyed watching her clumsy little hands explore the old puppet.

I know in my heart this will be my last Christmas. At times, I can feel my heart flutter, beating in fits and starts with an uneven rhythm. But I am not afraid of my death. I have no regrets. My life seems to me like the Russian dolls I once saw in the market. A smaller doll nested inside the larger, a still smaller doll inside that one, and another and another until the last tiny doll emerged. I am like that doll. I am now Anastasia the old woman, but I contain inside me all the other Anastasias—the schoolgirl; the loving daughter and sister; the tailor's apprentice; the proud businesswoman;

the jilted lover; the unwed mother; the strong, unashamed, abandoned lover; the mother who never married; the one who perseveres to the end. They all live inside the shriveled body of an old woman. I am all those Anastasias.

My book of days is finished. I am at peace.

AUTHOR'S NOTE

Anastasia Burkart, my great-great grandmother, was born April 12, 1796 and died May 10, 1873. Her death certificate lists her occupation as "day laborer," as anyone's doing piece work would have been. The cause of death was listed as "old age weakness."

I have constructed this story from the facts as I know them. Names, dates, and personal histories of family members are as accurate as I could determine. The details of German history are, to the best of my knowledge, also factual. Of course, much of the story cannot be known factually. My mission was to imagine how those facts, dates, and people would have affected a never-married mother of three in the context of her social and historical milieu.

Thank you, Anastasia, for allowing me to tell your story. I hope, even with its inevitable inaccuracies, I have done it justice.

CPSIA information can be obtained
at www.ICGtesting.com
Printed in the USA
LVHW091523210719
624773LV00004B/490/P